"I'll remind you what I said at my interview, Joel,"

Chesnie continued. "That I am not, repeat not, remotely interested in marriage!" She'd been spurred on by a growing niggle of annoyance— but she didn't regret a word of it.

Until Joel's brow went up and he exclaimed, "Marriage! Philip offered you marriage?"

"What on earth did you think he proposed?" Chesnie exclaimed.

Joel looked at her, looked at her as if he was really seeing her. "Oh, Chesnie Cosgrove," he answered, a smile coming to his wonderful mouth, "looking at you, half a dozen offers spring to mind."

From boardroom...to bride and groom!

**A secret romance, a forbidden affair,
a thrilling attraction?**

Working side by side, nine to five—and beyond...
No matter how hard these couples try
to keep their relationships strictly professional,
romance is definitely on the agenda!

But will a date in the office diary
lead to an appointment at the altar?
Find out in this exciting new miniseries
from Harlequin Romance®.

Look out for
The Tycoon's Proposition (#3729)
by Rebecca Winters
on sale December 2002

A PROFESSIONAL MARRIAGE

Jessica Steele

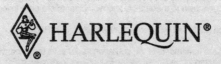

TORONTO • NEW YORK • LONDON
AMSTERDAM • PARIS • SYDNEY • HAMBURG
STOCKHOLM • ATHENS • TOKYO • MILAN • MADRID
PRAGUE • WARSAW • BUDAPEST • AUCKLAND

ISBN 0-373-03721-X

A PROFESSIONAL MARRIAGE

First North American Publication 2002.

CHAPTER ONE

'MR DAVENPORT will see you now.'

Chesnie's insides had been on the fidget for the last half-hour and now renewed their churning. But she rose elegantly to her feet and maintained her cool exterior and followed Barbara Platt—the woman whose job she was hoping to secure for herself—into the adjoining office.

'Chesnie Cosgrove.' Barbara Platt introduced her to the tall, dark-blond-haired man who was rising from his chair.

'Thank you, Barbara.' He had a pleasant, well-modulated voice, but as his present PA went out and closed the door Chesnie noted that there was something about the thirty-six or thirty-seven-year-old man who turned his blue gaze on her that said he could be exceedingly tough if the occasion demanded it. 'Take a seat, Miss Cosgrove,' he invited, in one sweeping glance taking in her slim five feet nine inches of height, her immaculate business suit, her red-blonde hair, green eyes and what one of her sisters had called her 'pale, flawless complexion to die for'. 'You found us without any trouble?' Joel Davenport opened pleasantly.

The vast offices of Yeatman Trading would be hard to miss. 'Yes,' she replied evenly, and that was all the time he had available for pleasantries, it seemed, for in the next split second her job interview with him was underway.

'So—tell me about yourself,' he opened.

'My qualifications are—'

'Were I unaware of your three years' experience as a senior secretary, your excellent typing speeds, and—according to your previous employer—your outstanding or-

ganising and communication skills, you wouldn't be sitting
here,' he cut her off.

Did she really want this job? He *was* tough! She'd had
a couple of interviews with Human Resources before she'd
got this far; clearly there was nothing about her business
background that hadn't been passed on to this man. She
wondered about going back to Cambridge to work—but
hadn't she made up her mind to make a complete break?
She decided to give Joel Davenport another chance.

'I'm twenty-five,' she informed him, and managed to
stay outwardly cool when she realised that if he'd seen her
application—and he seemed the kind of man who left nothing to chance—then he already knew that. 'I've been working in Cambridge.' He already knew that too. Stay cool,
Chesnie, stay cool. The fact was, though, that she didn't
know what she could add to what he already knew; her
second interview had been thorough in the extreme. She
stared at him, this man she was hoping to work for, green
eyes staring frankly into blue, and, feeling defeated, asked
the only question possible. 'What would you like to know?'

He studied her, not a smile in sight. She'd had more
appreciative glances. 'You're well qualified. Your reference
from your last employer is little short of glowing. Lionel
Browning obviously thought the world of you.'

'And I him,' she answered. Lionel Browning had been
an absolute darling to work for. A touch muddle-headed,
true, which was why he had left so much to her—and which
would all stand her in very good stead were she lucky
enough to land this job.

'Why then leave?'

Chesnie opened her mouth to trot out the same reason
she had given Human Resources: advancement in her career. To a certain extent that was true. But, had matters not
come to a head when Lionel's son, Hector, had decided to
come into the business she didn't know if she would ever
have been able to leave muddle-headed Lionel to run things
on his own. But suddenly she found she did not want to lie

to this direct-looking man. 'I'd been thinking for some time that I wouldn't mind something more challenging to get my teeth into,' she began truthfully.

'But…?'

She looked back at Joel Davenport. He was cool, cooler than she. And he was sharp—my word, he was sharp. He *knew*, for all she was sure she hadn't slipped up anywhere, that there was more to it than that.

'But I probably wouldn't have been able to leave Lionel had it not been for his son coming into the business.' She halted, too late regretting she had let this tough-looking man see she had a softer side when it came to her ex-employer. 'Hector Browning's own firm went bust. So he decided he'd come and give his father a hand.'

'You didn't get on?'

'It was part of my job to get on with everyone,' Chesnie answered, not taking kindly to having her professionalism questioned.

'So what went wrong?'

She had an idea this interview was going very badly, and decided she'd got nothing to lose by telling that which, hurt and humiliated, she had not told another living soul. 'Everything!' she answered evenly, adjusting her position on her chair, catching the flick of his glance to her long slender and shapely legs now neatly crossed at the ankles. 'On the same day I heard from my landlord that he'd decided to sell the property—and, no desperate rush, but would I care to look for a flat elsewhere?—I had a row with Hector Browning.'

'You usually row with the people you work with?'

'Lionel and I never had a cross word!' Chesnie retorted—and inwardly groaned. She'd be having a row with Joel Davenport any minute! And she wasn't working with him, or for him—or ever!

He was unperturbed. 'Hector Browning rubbed you up the wrong way?'

'That I could, and did, cope with. What I was not pre-

pared to stay and put up with was that—was that...' Joel
Davenport waited, saying not one word, which left her
forced to continue. 'From the various snide remarks Hector
Browning had made I knew he resented my closeness to
his father, my affection for him and his affection for me.
He—Hector...' Again she hesitated, but the fact that she
knew herself innocent made her tilt her chin a fraction.
'When he that day accused me of having an affair with his
father,' she made herself go on, 'I knew that one of us
would have to go. Blood being thicker than water, I also
knew it would be me.'

'You handed in your resignation.'

'I left last week—the end of the month.'

'And were you?' Joel Davenport asked.

'Was I what?'

'Having an affair with his father?'

Her eyes widened in surprise and annoyance that anyone
could ask such a thing. Somehow, though, she was able to
maintain the outer cool she showed to the world. 'No, I
was not!' she stated clearly, and, not wishing to say any
more on the subject, she left it there.

To his credit, Joel Davenport allowed her to do so. He
nodded, at any rate—she took it that he believed her. 'Human Resources will have explained the package that goes
with the position.' He took the interview into another area.
'Obviously the salary, pension and holiday entitlement are
acceptable to you or you wouldn't have proceeded with
your application.'

'It's a very generous package,' Chesnie stated calmly.
Generous! It was a sensational salary!

'The successful candidate will earn every part of it,' he
replied, which she felt hinted that she was not the successful candidate. Though when he continued she began to
wonder... 'The job as my PA demands one hundred per
cent commitment,' he advised her, and surprised her by
adding, 'Your qualifications aside, you're a beautiful

woman, Miss Cosgrove—' he did not seem personally impressed '—and no doubt have many admirers.'

About to deny she had any, Chesnie, who just wasn't interested in relationships, suddenly felt feminine enough to want to go along with his view that she had a constant stream of admirers at her door. 'They wouldn't interfere with my work,' she replied.

'I may need you to work away with me on occasion,' he went on. She knew from the job description that there were times when Joel Davenport required his PA to accompany him on overnight stays when he visited their Glasgow offices, and had no problem whatsoever with that. 'Supposing such an occasion arose at short notice—say, half an hour before a theatre date with your favourite man?'

'I'd hope my favourite man would enjoy the theatre just as much without me,' she replied promptly, and thought she caught a momentary twitch of her serious interviewer's mouth—quite a nice-shaped mouth, she suddenly realised—but it was come and gone in an instant.

'There's no one man in particular in your life?'

'No,' she replied. Who had the time? Or the inclination, for that matter?

'No marriage plans?' he asked sternly, her one-syllable answer insufficient, apparently. But she resented his question. She hadn't asked him if he was married or about to be! She studied him for a moment. Good-looking, a director of the expanded and still expanding multi-national Yeatman Trading—he had it all, which no doubt included some lovely wife somewhere.

Suddenly she became aware that as she was studying him, so keen blue eyes were studying her. 'I'm not remotely interested in marriage,' she stated bluntly, belatedly realising his question, in light of his statement that the job as his PA demanded one hundred per cent commitment, was perhaps a valid one.

'You sound as if you've something against marriage,' he commented.

With her parents and her sisters as fine examples, who wouldn't have? Chesnie kept her thoughts to herself. 'I believe the latest statistics show that forty per cent of marriages end in divorce. Personally, I'm more career-oriented than marriage-minded.'

He nodded, but when she was expecting some comment on her reply, he instead enquired, 'You're still living in Cambridge?'

'For the moment. Though at present I'm staying with my sister, here in London, for a few days.'

'You're obviously prepared to move here. Have you found anywhere to live yet?'

'I thought I'd better sort out a job first,' she answered, and was surprised when, without a response, he got to his feet.

'Perhaps you should set about finding your accommodation without delay,' he suggested pleasantly.

Chesnie looked at him. Clearly the interview was over. She stood up as he came round his desk. She was wearing two and a half inch heels and still had to look up at him. 'I'm not sure...' she faltered, not at all sure she should believe what she thought he was saying.

He held out his right hand, and automatically her right hand met his warm, firm clasp. 'I should like you to start on Monday, Chesnie,' he confirmed, and for the first time he smiled.

Chesnie managed to keep her face straight while she was in the Yeatman Trading building, but once she had left the building so too did she leave her cool, sophisticated image, her lovely face splitting into an equally lovely grin. She'd got it! She'd jolly well got it! Only then did she acknowledge how very much she had wanted this job as PA to Joel Davenport.

It sounded hard work—she thrived on hard work. To be constantly busy had been her lifeline. She hadn't been sure what sort of work she wanted to do when she had left school, but with her studies finished and no need to spend time at her desk in her room she had spent more time with her parents. Their constant sniping at each other had driven her to take various courses at evening classes, all to do with business management.

It seemed to her she had been brought up in a house full of strife. The youngest of four sisters, with a two-year gap separating each of them, she had been twelve when her eldest sister, Nerissa, had married—for the first time. Nerissa was now on her second marriage, but that didn't appear to be any happier than her first. Chesnie's second sister, Robina, had married next—she was always leaving her husband and returning for weeks on end to the home she had confided she had only married young to get away from.

When her sister Tonia married, Chesnie had thought surely it must be third time lucky for one of her sisters. But, no. Tonia had produced two babies in quick succession and seemed to have quickly developed the same love-hate relationship with her husband that her parents shared.

With one or other of her sisters forever returning in tears to the family home, to rail against the man she had married, Chesnie had soon known that she wanted no part in marriage. She had attended college most evenings, doing most of her studying at the weekends. She had not lacked for potential boyfriends, however, and occasionally had gone out on a date with either someone she had known previously or had met at college. On occasions, too, she had experimented with a little kissing, but as soon as things had looked like getting serious she'd put up barriers.

She'd become aware she had started to get a reputation for being aloof. It had not bothered her—nor had it seemed to stop men asking her for a date.

Chesnie had been working in an office for two years when her studies came to an end. She'd taken more courses, and done more study, and two years later had been ready to take a better-paid job. She'd changed firms and begun work as a secretary and she'd been good at it.

What she had not been so good at was handling the traumatic friction that seemed to be a constant feature in her family home. She'd told herself she was being oversensitive and that everyone had their ups and downs. The only trouble was that in her fraught home, the animosity was permanent.

Having been brought up to be self-sufficient, she had thought often of leaving and had soon felt she could just about afford a bedsit somewhere. Only the knowledge that her mother would be furious should she leave her commodious and graceful home for some lowly bedsit had stopped her.

Matters had come to a head one weekend, however, when all three weeping sisters, and crying babies, had descended. From where Chesnie had viewed it, each sister had been trying to outdo the other with reports of what a rotten husband her spouse was.

When Chesnie had felt her sympathy for the trio turning into a feeling of weariness with all three of them, she'd gone out into the garden and found her father inspecting his roses.

'You came to escape the bedlam too?' he asked wryly.

'Dad, I'm thinking of moving out.' The words she hadn't rehearsed came blurting from her.

'I think I'll come with you,' he replied. But, glancing at her to see if she was smiling at his quip, he saw that she wasn't. 'You're serious, aren't you?' he asked.

The words were out; she couldn't retract them. 'I've been thinking of it for some while. I'm sure I could manage a small bedsit, and...'

'You'd better make that a small flat, and in a good area, if you want me to have any peace.'

Two days later her mother sought her out. 'Your father tells me your home isn't good enough for you any more.'

Chesnie knew that she loved her mother—just as she knew the futility of arguing with her. 'I'd like to be—more—independent,' she replied quietly.

Ten days after that, and much to her astonishment, her mother told her she had found somewhere for her. Chesnie was so overjoyed that her mother, having slept on it, had decided to aid her rather than make life difficult, that she closed her eyes to the fact that the rent of the flat was far more than she could afford.

Furnishing the flat was no problem. What with bits and pieces from her parents and her grandparents, and with her restless sister Nerissa always changing her home around and getting rid of some item of furniture or other, Chesnie soon made her small flat very comfortable.

She had been resident for two months, though, when she had to face up to the reality that she just couldn't afford to be that independent. Her mother would be horrified if she went downmarket and found herself a bedsit. And from Chesnie's point of view she would be horrified herself if she had to give up the peace and quiet she had found to return to her old home.

When Browning Enterprises advertised for a senior secretary she applied for the job, and got it. It paid more, and she earned it when she started taking on more and more responsibility. The only fly in the ointment was Lionel Browning's son. But Hector Browing had his own business, and apart from visits to his father, usually when Hector's finances needed a cash injection, Chesnie saw little of him. She was aware that he resented her, but could think of no reason for his dislike other than the fact that he knew that *she* knew he was as near broke as made no difference.

She was happy living in a place of her own, but since she lived in the same town as her parents she popped in to see them every two or three weeks—and always came away glad she had made the decision to leave.

Then, a year later, her paternal grandmother died, and after months of living in a kind of vacuum her grandfather sold his home in Herefordshire and, with her parents having ample room, moved in with them.

Chesnie adored her grandfather. She seemed to have a

special affinity with him, and had feared from the beginning that life with her bickering parents would not suit her peace-loving Gramps. She took to 'popping in' to her old home more frequently.

She knew he looked forward to her visits, and knew when he suggested he teach her to drive that he was looking for excuses to get out of the house.

She and her grandfather spent many pleasant Saturday afternoons together, and when she passed her driving test she took to taking him for a drive somewhere. Three months ago she had driven him across country to Herefordshire, and to the village where he had lived prior to moving in with her parents.

Six days later she had arrived home from her office to find her grandfather sitting outside her flat in his car. 'I'm not such a good cook as my mother, but you're welcome to come to dinner,' she invited lightly, watching him, knowing from the fact of him being there as much from the excited light in his eyes that something a touch monumental was going on.

Over macaroni cheese and salad he told her he had noticed a 'To Let' sign in the garden of a small cottage on their visit to his home village last Saturday. He hadn't phoned the agent because, knowing the owner, he had phoned him instead. The result being the tenancy was his straight away on a temporary let while he waited for something in the village to come up for sale.

What could she say? 'It's what you want, Gramps?' she asked quietly.

'I should never have left,' he answered simply, and she could only think, since he had never parted with his furniture but had put it in store, that perhaps without knowing it he had always meant to return.

'What do my parents think?'

A wicked light she hadn't seen in a long while entered his eyes. 'Your father's all right about it—er—your mother's taken it personally.'

Chesnie knew all about her mother taking it 'personally'—she would go on and on about it, and Chesnie suspected he would want to move out sooner rather than later. 'When are you leaving?' she asked.

'I was wondering if you're free to drive me there tomorrow?' he asked, looking positively cheeky.

He had got everything arranged so quickly! She had to grin. 'I'd love to,' she answered, and was thinking in terms of availability of trains for the return trip when her grandfather seemed to read her mind.

'You wouldn't care to look after my car for me, would you? I'll seldom need it, and it will only be until I can find a property in the village with a garage. There isn't one at the cottage.'

That had been three months ago. Chesnie missed her grandfather but had driven to see him several times. When, six weeks ago, Hector Browning had accused her of having an affair with his father she had known she couldn't possibly work at Browning Enterprises any longer.

Knowing she was going to part company with Lionel Browning, and having just received a letter asking her to vacate her flat, it had been decision time. She needed somewhere new to live and work; she could do both anywhere.

When Chesnie had seen the advert for the PA's job at Yeatman Trading, and subsequently passed the first and second interviews, she'd crossed her fingers and hoped...

She still had a wide grin on her face when she drove up to the smart appartment block where her sister lived. She had a new job now, PA to none other than Mr Joel Davenport himself.

Nerissa was in, took one look at her beaming face, and squealed, 'You got it!'

Later she calmed down enough to say that she had known she would get it. 'The rest of us had to get married to afford to leave home. But not you, clever girl, you inherited the family brain.' From Chesnie's viewpoint it hadn't been that easy. She had worked hard, but Nerissa was going blithely on, 'Now to sort you out with a flat. Stephen was having a word with someone last night who may have something—' She broke off waspishly. 'He does have his uses.'

From that moment on everything seemed to move at lightning pace. Chesnie was not a partying person, but Nerissa made her promise to return for a party she and Stephen were holding on Saturday evening, and Chesnie returned to Cambridge and packed up her belongings ready for her move.

The party was a success; Nerissa wouldn't have had it any other way. But, although Chesnie found the function enjoyable, she had other things on her mind—she had only two weeks to work alongside Joel Davenport's present PA and get up to speed. It wasn't very long—would she cope?

Chesnie arrived back at her sister's apartment after her first Monday in her new job with her head spinning—and a sinking feeling that two months, let alone two weeks, wouldn't be long enough for her to remember all that there was to absorb.

She was ready for bed and didn't think she had energy enough to eat a meal. Her sister had other plans. 'How was your first day?' she asked straight away.

'I'm on my knees!' Chesnie confessed.

'That good, huh? And how was the new boss?'

'I haven't seen him. He's in Scotland until Wednesday.'

'Right, now, don't take your jacket off. The flat Stephen told me about has come up. Come on, we'll go and take a look.'

Somewhere to live was a priority. From somewhere Chesnie conjured up some enthusiasm and, with her sister driving, went to view a small flat on the outskirts of the city.

The flat consisted of a sitting room, bathroom, a tiny kitchen and two bedrooms, though the second bedroom was no bigger than her parents' broom cupboard. 'If there's a chance, I'll take it,' Chesnie declared at once. The rent was astronomical—but so too was her salary.

'You're sure?' Nerissa questioned. 'You're welcome to stay with me for as long as you like—if you can put up with Tibbetts.' 'Tibbetts' being her husband, Stephen Tibbetts.

'This will do fine,' Chesnie assured her, and in no time Nerissa was speaking to her husband on the phone.

'You can move in any time,' she said the moment she had ended her call. 'Let's celebrate!'

Chesnie was grateful that the celebration was nothing more than a meal out with a glass of wine.

Tuesday proved every bit as busy as the previous day, with Barbara Platt trying to break her in gently but as aware as Chesnie that there was not too much time remaining before Barbara departed a week on Friday.

Joel Davenport had already been at his desk for over an hour when Chesnie arrived at her office on Wednesday. She was not late, was in fact fifteen minutes early. In the short time she'd been there she had heard that he simply ate up work—throughout that day he proved it.

Not that she had much to do with him. Though he did leave his office at one point to speak to Barbara and to pause in passing to ask, pleasantly enough, 'Settling in?'

She raised her head, maintaining her cool image to politely agree, 'Yes, thank you,' and he went on to Barbara's desk and Chesnie went back to what she had been doing.

By Friday, although she was starting to grow more confident that she was up to the job, she was nevertheless mentally exhausted by the time she arrived at her sister's home, to be greeted by Nerissa smilingly telling her, 'Philip Pomeroy rang. He wants to take you out.'

'You make me sound like a set of dentures! Who's Philip Pomeroy?'

'You're hopeless!' Nerissa complained. 'You met him at my party last Saturday. Tallish, wavy brownish hair, very slightly receding, pushing forty. Ring any bells?'

Chesnie did a mental flip back to the party, and placed Philip Pomeroy as a rather amiable man, interested in her, but inoffensive with it. 'Did you tell him I was busy?'

'I told him you'd ring him.'

'Nerissa!'

'Oh, go on, ring him. He's nice.'

Out of courtesy to her sister, who had promised a return phone call on her behalf, Chesnie reluctantly phoned Philip Pomeroy, who appeared pleased she had rung and straight away asked her to dine with him.

'I'm very busy at the moment,' she replied.

'You're too busy to eat?'

'I'm moving into a new flat tomorrow,' she explained. 'It will take me over a week to get everything unpacked.'

'I could bring champagne and caviar round, and we could snack while you unpack.'

She laughed and decided she liked him. 'Some other time,' she said, and rang off.

Chesnie had a change from mental exhaustion on Saturday, when she met the delivery van from Cambridge and set about placing her belongings and hanging up curtains.

On Monday Barbara Platt afforded her the most wonderful, if scary, compliment by telling her that Joel Davenport had a meeting at one of their other businesses and that Barbara was going with him. 'We won't be back again today, but I know you'll cope.'

Chesnie wished she had Barbara's confidence in that, but, to her delight—though bearing in mind it had gone seven in the evening before she finally switched off her computer—cope she did. She was not complaining—she was starting to really enjoy her job. She went home to her new flat feeling on top of the world.

Friday, Barbara's last day, arrived all too quickly. Chesnie spent the morning eagerly absorbing all and everything that Barbara was telling her of the more confidential details of their work. She supposed that with Barbara divulging such matters it must mean that she had satisfied herself that the new PA was worthy of such confidences.

Feeling enormously pleased with Barbara's trust, Chesnie was further delighted when at half past twelve the good-looking Joel Davenport came into their office and, instead of going over to Barbara's desk, came over to Chesnie.

'I'm taking my number one PA for an extended lunch. The office is all yours, Chesnie Cosgrove.'

Indeed, so delighted was she at this further show of trust in her abilities that her cool exterior slipped momentarily. She smiled, a natural smile. *'Bon appétit,'* she replied.

She became aware that Joel Davenport was staring at her as if seeing something new in her for the first time, but before she could change her smile back to her more usual guarded smile he muttered, 'Those incredibly long eyelashes can't be real.'

'I'm afraid they are,' she replied.

'Amazing,' he commented—and took his 'number one' PA off for a parting lunch.

Feeling a mite disturbed by Joel Davenport's personal comment—even if it had sounded more matter-of-fact than personal—Chesnie was soon over any disquiet when she realised that if Barbara was his number one PA today, then on Monday yours truly, Chesnie Cosgrove, would be number one!

She had plenty to do, and was fully involved in her work when at five to three Barbara came back from what it transpired had been a champagne lunch.

'Joel has gone on to keep his three o'clock appointment,' Barbara explained. 'Now, what can I help you with?'

'I think you've filled in as many blanks as you can,' Chesnie replied.

And guessed she must have sounded a mite apprehensive when Barbara replied that she was confident she would cope admirably. 'A bit different from your predecessor.'

'My predecessor?' Chesnie was puzzled. Mustard had nothing on Joel Davenport's present PA.

'Didn't I mention it?' Barbara realised that she hadn't, and went on to correct that oversight.

Apparently Barbara's life had changed dramatically when she had met Derek Platt. In no time she had fallen in love and married him. Derek had been in the process of purchasing a small holding in the Welsh borders, and that had been fine by Barbara. A smart and mature woman, she'd looked forward to this change of lifestyle.

'I gave ample notice, and we thought we'd selected the right person. But she proved not up to the job, and Joel didn't think the other candidates were any better, so we advertised again. And—' she smiled '—here you are. And, I'm certain, more than up to the job.'

Chesnie fervently hoped she was right. 'That won't prevent you from leaving me your phone number, I hope?' It had been Barbara's suggestion that she would. But she laughed and, having more or less cleared her desk, began to expand on matters other than the work which Chesnie would be dealing with.

Barbara was full of praise for Joel. Yeatman Trading had been going through a very tough time when he had joined the firm. He had seen at once what needed to be done, and had done it—had transformed the company—and been rewarded with a seat on the board.

'And now,' Barbara continued, 'within the next year Winslow Yeatman is going to retire.'

'The chairman?' Chesnie had picked that up from somewhere during the past two weeks.

'None other,' Barbara agreed. 'And Joel wants that job— very badly. He has very progressive ideas, and believes that to be able to put those ideas into effect he needs to be chairman.'

'Will he get it?' Chesnie asked.

'If there's any justice he will,' Barbara answered. 'It's largely through his efforts that a firm that was heading for the rocks has gone from strength to strength this past ten years. He, more than anyone, is responsible for its growth and expansion. He's ambitious and hard-headed when it comes to business. But he's good. They certainly don't come any better.'

Chesnie had seen that much for herself in the short time she'd been there. 'You think he might not get it?' she asked.

'Nothing's certain. The problem here is that this started off as a family firm a hundred or so years ago, and, although new blood such as Joel has gradually infiltrated, over half the board are family members. Three of whom I know for a fact want a Yeatman to head the company. There are nine people on the board, excluding the chairman, and while I know there are three of the directors who are for Joel, he can't vote for himself, so that leaves two other votes as yet unaccounted for. Should the vote be split and Winslow Yeatman have to make the casting vote then it's more than likely he'll favour a family man.'

'One of his family?'

Barbara shook her head. 'A man with a family. He also wants what is best for the firm.'

'Doesn't J... Mr Davenport have a family?'

'He's not married.'

Chesnie felt a little surprised. 'Some woman named Felice phoned for him last week, and a woman named Gina phoned to speak to him on Monday. I put them in the wife and daughter slot.'

'Girlfriends.' Barbara corrected Chesnie's assumption. 'He's *more* than happy with his bachelor lifestyle.' She gave a wicked grin. 'Though his fellow director, Arlene Enderby, née Yeatman, recently divorced, non-working but taking her cut just the same—and who just happens to be the chairman's niece—has got her eye on Joel.'

'Does he know?'

Barbara gave a whoop of laughter. 'I've an idea that there's not much that goes on in the female mind that Joel doesn't know. He's taken her out a couple of times, so I'm positive she will have filled in any gaps.' At that point Barbara seemed to collect herself. 'And I'm talking too much—must be the champage—I'm not used to it. Either that or some instinctive feeling that you'll be better able to help him get what he deserves and has worked for if you know more of what's going on.'

At a quarter to five Joel Davenport, who must have entered his office by the outer door, rang for Barbara to go in to see him. She came out ten minutes later, emotional tears in her eyes, a cheque in one hand, a jeweller's box in the other, and a gorgeous bouquet of flowers in her arms.

'Oh, Chesnie,' she said, emotion still with her after the presentation she had just received, 'I do so hope you'll be as happy working here as I have been.'

'I'm sure I shall,' Chesnie answered with a smile, but more hoped that she could do the job. For, aside from the everyday difficulties and stress that were part and parcel of the job, from what Barbara had said earlier it seemed there was a lot of in-fighting going on too.

For a fact, there were three board members who were against Joel Davenport getting the chairman's job.

Chesnie suddenly felt swallowed up by an unexpected huge wave of loyalty, and she determined that if there was any small thing in her power she could do to help him get that chairman's job, she would do it. Then she laughed at herself. What on earth did she think she, a PA, could do that would help when it came to electing the new chairman?

CHAPTER TWO

IT WAS four weeks since Barbara had left, and Chesnie was thankful that in those four weeks she had not had to phone Barbara or needed to call on the services of Eileen Gray, a kind of floating PA who, while not wanting the pressure of being anyone's full-time PA, was so good at the job that the company did not want to let her go.

Chesnie drove to work that Monday four weeks after Barbara's departure and for the first time truly believed that she *could* do the job of Joel's number one PA.

It had not been an easy four weeks. Joel Davenport, for all he made his job seem effortless, had an appetite for work that at first had caused her to work in overdrive just to try and keep up with him.

She worked late; once, when he was out for the day, staying at the office until gone nine at night to catch up and so have her desk clear for the next morning.

Most evenings she staggered home to make a quick snack, get her smart business clothes ready for the morning, and fall into bed. Sometimes she dreamed of him, but that was hardly surprising; he had become a dominant force in her life.

On one weekend she had visited her grandfather in Herefordshire, and another weekend she'd gone to see her parents in Cambridge. Robina had been there, having left Ronnie for a 'final' time. She was divorcing him, she'd declared in floods of tears, she'd had enough. Ronnie had phoned, and there were more tears as Robina had screeched a list of his faults down the phone at him.

All that hate and recrimination had served only to freshly endorse for Chesnie that she'd got the better bargain when she'd decided never to marry. Though she had to smile—when would she get the chance? Working for and with such a high-powered, work-oriented man, she didn't have the time to date, much less to build any kind of relationship.

Which reminded her. Nerissa had telephoned last night to say Philip Pomeroy had rung again and could he have her sister's number?

'You didn't give it to him?' Chesnie had asked, guessing that Philip wanted to ask her out; she didn't have time to go out. By not letting him have her newly connected number, she was spared having to make excuses.

'I promised you I wouldn't,' Nerissa had confirmed.

With her new-found confidence in her ability to cope with her job, Chesnie parked her grandfather's car, swung into the building and took the lift to the top floor. It went without saying that Joel Davenport would already be hard at work. Unless he was out of town he was always in before her.

An involuntary smile lit her mouth as she recalled that first Monday after Barbara had gone. Hoping to look as cool and as poised as she was striving to look, Chesnie, feeling a bundle of nerves, had entered her office. No sooner had she sat down, though, and Joel Davenport had come to greet her as if it had been her first day.

'Good morning, Chesnie,' he'd said pleasantly. 'We haven't frightened you off, then?'

She had given him her guarded smile. 'Good morning, Mr Davenport,' she'd replied and, inwardly churning, 'I don't scare easily,' she had added.

He'd studied her, nodded, and then commented, 'That's what I like to hear. The name's Joel,' he indicated, and her first day as *numero uno* had begun.

The door between the two offices stood open today, as it sometimes did when she went in. 'Good morning,' Chesnie called to the dark-blond-haired man absorbed in the paperwork in front of him.

'Good morning,' he answered, but did not raise his head. Business as usual.

Chesnie had barely stowed her bag when Darren, the post boy, arrived. 'Good morning, Miss Cosgrove,' he said huskily, and as their hands touched as she relieved him of the bundles of post he blushed crimson.

Chesnie took her eyes from him, giving him time to compose himself. 'How's your mother?' she asked. 'I do hope she's on the mend.' She glanced at him, glad to see his blush had died down.

'She's going back to work today,' he answered on a gulp of breath. 'Thank you,' he added, and gave her a beautiful smile as his eyes glued to her face, he backed to the door.

Then he became aware that Joel Davenport had come from his office and was standing watching him—Darren bolted. 'That young man idolises you,' Joel said abruptly.

'It's only a crush,' Chesnie replied, and was ready to deal with any query her employer had when she discovered he wasn't ready to dismiss the subject yet.

'He'll never get over it while you treat him that way!'

What way was that? 'I'd rather be pleasant to him than not,' she answered, as calmly as she was able.

'Is that the way you treat all your admirers?'

What had this got to do with work? 'It depends how old they are,' she replied evenly. 'Young men like Darren, sensitive young men, deserve to have their blushes respected. Older, more cynical men,' she went on, looking one such straight in the eye, 'are too tough to need kid-glove treatment.'

A grunt was her answer. 'Bring the post through when you've sorted it!' he rapped.

Yes, sir, three bags full, sir. And, anyhow, he could talk! In the short time she'd been there she'd observed he had quite a fan club amongst the female staff.

The morning that had got off to a rancorous start did not improve much for Chesnie when, nearing one o'clock, Joel's office door opened. Observing he wasn't there, the most striking-looking blue-eyed brunette, sporting a sensational tan, fluttered through and into Chesnie's office.

'You must be Chesnie!' She smiled. 'Uncle Winslow told me all about you.'

'Uncle Winslow' must be Winslow Yeatman, the chairman. Chesnie had by then met him several times and found him a most charming gentleman. 'You must be Arlene Enderby,' Chesnie guessed—the non-working director of the company.

'You have it. I've come to take Joel to lunch, but he doesn't appear to be in.'

Chesnie, who managed Joel's diary with keen efficiency, knew for certain he did not have a lunch appointment with the chairman's niece. 'He's probably been held up somewhere,' she suggested tactfully. 'Perhaps...'

'Oh, we haven't arranged lunch. I've just got back from soaking up the sun on holiday.' She almost purred as she trotted out, 'We have such a lot to catch up on, I thought—' She broke off to exclaim, 'Ah!' as they heard a door open and saw Joel stride into his office. 'Joel! *Darling!*' Arlene Enderby cried, and was in the other office, flinging her arms around him as if he was some long-lost lover.

Chesnie met the eyes of her employer as Arlene Enderby snuggled into his arms. Chesnie did not smile; neither did he. She got up and deliberately closed the door—and discovered she was inwardly shaking, experiencing the strangest sensation of not caring to see him with his arms around some woman. How odd! Why should it bother her at all?

It wasn't in the least odd, she decided a moment later. This was a place of business and that was why she didn't care for it. Everything that happened in this office should be purely professional. Which wasn't what was happening next door. What *was* happening next door? It was very quiet in there. She half wished she had left the door open.

Chesnie was over the slight glitch in her equilibrium by the next day. She smiled and chatted lightly to Darren when he brought the post, and dealt pleasantly with the various heads of department—male ones—who seemed to find it necessary to stop by her desk for one reason or another. She had gradually got to know more and more of the people within the organisation, and it was good to be able to put a face to the various names that cropped up from time to time.

Though there was one new face she hadn't seen before. The tall white-haired man poked his head round her office door at a quarter to one and came in. 'Well, you're a decided improvement on Barbara Thingy,' he beamed, and, when Chesnie looked pleasantly enquiring, asked, 'Is my son around?'

'You're Joel's father?'

'I know, I know. I don't look old enough to have a son that age,' quipped the man Chesnie thought must be at least seventy. 'Magnus Davenport, at your service.' He extended his right hand, and Chesnie immediately decided she liked him.

'Chesnie Cosgrove,' she introduced herself, shaking his hand. 'I'm afraid your son is at a business lunch. Can I help you at all?'

'Oh, dear, that's a nuisance! I've driven all the way across the city hoping he'd take *me* to lunch,' Davenport Senior replied with a sigh.

Chesnie thought for a moment. The matter was settled when it came to her that Joel's father was only about ten years younger than Gramps. She wouldn't hesitate to take her grandfather to lunch. 'I'll take you if you like?' she offered.

'I thought you'd never ask!' he beamed.

Over lunch she discovered Magnus Davenport was a bit of a rascal. He insisted that she call him by his first name, but as he chatted away freely, about everything and everyone, she found that as well as being an outrageous gossip he was also a bit of a flirt—but quite harmless.

He openly told her that his wife, Joel's mother, had thrown him out and divorced him years ago. 'Said I was

shiftless. Can you believe that? And that she'd had enough.'
Chesnie was on the point of feeling sorry for him when all
of a sudden he laughed. 'D'you know, I can't really blame
her? I never did hold down a job for long. Come to think
of it, one of the happiest days I've had was when I retired.'

Chesnie had to laugh too; he had a sort of infectious
quality about him. 'I must think about getting back,' she
hinted, when he seemed inclined to linger over his coffee.

'I'm going to the races tomorrow. Fancy coming with
me?' he asked.

She smiled and declined, and knew she was going to be
late when Magnus Davenport drove her back to the
Yeatman Trading building. She was not unduly alarmed
that it was nearer half past two than two o'clock when
Magnus dropped her off. She had worked late many times,
and would cheerfully work late tonight if she hadn't finished her workload by five.

'I won't come in—give me a call if you change your
mind about the races,' he said, and handed her his card.

Chesnie was smiling as she bade him goodbye, but had
work on her mind as she opened the door to her office. She
noticed at once that the communicating door to her employer's office was open and that Joel was back from his
business lunch.

Courtesy demanded that she commented on her lateness.
She crossed that carpet and was aware that Joel knew she
had returned, even though she hadn't noticed him look up.

Nor did he glance up then, when she stood to the side
of his desk. For some reason it niggled her. She'd be
blessed if she'd say a word till he acknowledged her pres-
ence.

Just as she was about to turn around and go back to her
office, however, he carefully laid down his pen. Then his
head came up. He leaned back in his chair, silently ap-
praising her, from the top of her red-blonde hair, to her
slender but curvy figure in the royal blue suit, and all the
way down to her shoes. Then, while she was studying his

firm jaw, noticing that his mouth was pretty terrific even
without the semblance of a smile, he moved his glance
swiftly upwards and his blue eyes met her stubborn green
ones head on.

Good, she'd got his attention. He waited—waited for her
to speak first—and she felt quite irritated about that too.
But she had been at pains to adopt a cool front; she wasn't
about to let it slip now.

'Your father called,' she began evenly, pleasantly. 'He
was disappointed not to see you,' she added. 'We went to
lunch,' she informed him, when Davenport said nothing.

'No doubt you were able to help him over his disap-
pointment,' he threw in sourly, and at that moment pugi-
listic tendencies awakened in Chesnie that she'd had no
idea she possessed. To her amazement she felt a momentary
desire to poke Davenport Junior in the eye with something
sharp and painful. 'Who paid?' he asked abruptly, his tone
toughening.

What was it with him? The nerve! 'Your father was my
guest,' she answered primly.

'He conned you into taking him to lunch, didn't he?'

'Not at all. I liked him,' she began. 'He—'

'I'll reimburse you!' Joel Davenport cut in sharply—and
her anger went soaring, and with it her cool image.

'No, you won't!' she flared hotly, and saw him smile—
every bit as if he really enjoyed fracturing the cool front
she'd displayed this past six weeks.

He shrugged. 'So I won't,' he agreed, his tone all at once
silky, and picked up his pen.

Chesnie went swiftly back to her own office. She felt
then that she hated him. He'd done that on purpose—made
her forget her poise for a moment. She didn't want her front
fractured; it made her feel vulnerable. She did not care for
the feeling.

She slammed into her work and wanted nothing to do
with him. This was what happened when you let person-
alities in on the scene. Meeting his father, liking him,

laughing with him, had put a severe dent in the Chesnie Cosgrove she preferred to show the world. It seemed as if one Davenport had softened her up for another. Well, she wasn't having it.

By four that afternoon her cool exterior was firmly back in place. At four-fifteen Larry Jenkins from Accounts came into her office with a query that wasn't strictly in her domain, but she was pleased to be able to handle it. Though Larry didn't stay long when the door opened and Joel Davenport strode in.

Joel watched him hastily leave. 'I hear this corridor is alive with senior executives in need of guidance from you on some urgent matter or other,' he commented.

What was she supposed to answer to that? And how did he know? Though she supposed that not a lot got by him— even when he wasn't around! 'Is there something *you* need guidance with?' she enquired coolly of his visit—and didn't hate him any more when he actually laughed, as though the way she'd bounced that back at him had amused him.

'Are you still mad at me?' he asked, with such a wealth of natural charm there that she began to like him very much again.

'You deliberately provoked me!' she accused primly.

'Did I?' he asked innocently—and a moment later was all business and instruction.

Chesnie went home that night in a happy frame of mind. She liked her job, had never felt so stimulated by any work she had done before, and she liked her boss too. He was…Chesnie came to, to realise she had drifted off for quite some time to thinking of Joel Davenport, her good-looking boss. My, did he have it all. Gina had rung him this morning, but he hadn't stayed talking to her above a minute. Chesnie had an idea that Gina was on her way out.

Aware that her employer would be flying up to Scotland first thing on Thursday morning, Chesnie went into the office earlier than usual on Wednesday, so she could complete any information he needed to take with him before he left the office that night.

'Good morning,' she called as she went in, and hardly thought he would notice her early arrival.

'Couldn't sleep?'

She should have known better—there was no detail small enough that he'd miss. She grinned to herself and started her day.

She did not feel like grinning when, in Joel's office, taking notes later that morning, the phone on her desk rang. Saving time, Joel stretched out a hand and pressed a button to divert the call to his phone, and took the call himself.

Whoever it was had been put through to the right phone in the first place. 'Who wants her?' he demanded. And while Chesnie was thinking it must be some business call, because her family would only phone in the direst emergency, he was charmingly saying, 'I'm sorry, Pomeroy, my PA isn't available just now.' So saying, he put down the phone and terminated the call. Then, as cool as you like, he calmly carried on from where he had left off.

Feeling little short of amazed, Chesnie stared disbelievingly at her employer. Even while she was recognising that someone named Pomeroy had phoned to speak to her, and that the only Pomeroy she knew was Philip Pomeroy, Chesnie was astonished that Joel Davenport had not passed the call over to her.

She quickly found her voice. 'Anyone I should ring back?' she enquired politely, annoyance straining at the leash.

Joel looked across at her, his blue glance icy. 'How do you know Philip Pomeroy?' he demanded.

Ready to tell him it was none of his business, Chesnie decided that one of them should show some manners here. 'I met him at a party.' She forced the words out.

Joel grunted, didn't look impressed, and stated coldly, 'You *do* know he's with the opposition?'

'Opposition?'

'In case you didn't know he heads Symington Technology—our competitors in the technology field.'

'I didn't know,' Chesnie answered, and started to feel cross that Joel Davenport was as good as reminding her that the work she did for him was highly confidential. She resented that unsaid reminder, resented his icy manner, and tilted her chin a defiant fraction. 'You obviously know him better than I do,' she replied, her control back. And, knowing she was pushing it, 'Do you happen to have his number?'

Icy blue eyes bored into hers; she refused to back down. 'I shouldn't bother,' he replied shortly. 'He'll ring again.'

Chesnie was still silently mutinying against Joel Davenport when she went back to her desk. She didn't particularly wish to speak to Philip Pomeroy—and thank you, Nerissa, for telling him where I work—but that was for her to decide, not Davenport. He spoke to his girlfriends when they rang him at the office. Where did he get off not allowing her that same courtesy? Even if Philip Pomeroy *was* the opposition.

Chesnie was not feeling any more Davenport-friendly when, around midday, just as he had predicted, Philip Pomeroy rang again. Had the door between the two offices not been open, and Joel Davenport privy to everything she said, Chesnie might well have refused Philip's invitation to dinner. As it was, she knew full well he had heard her 'Hello, Philip' and would more than likely be tuned in. Stubbornly she determined that Davenport should know exactly what she thought of his offensive, if unspoken, reminder that her work was highly confidential.

'Say yes,' Philip was urging. 'You can't still be unpacking.'

She glanced through to the other office—Davenport appeared to be working, but she knew his capability to handle several things at once. 'I'd love to go out with you,' she heard herself reply—and loved it when Davenport turned his head to glance her way. He was unsmiling. She smiled—she couldn't help it—then dipped her head so he shouldn't see her smile, though she guessed he had.

'Tonight?' Philip was pressing. 'Give me your address and I'll pick you up at—'

'Er—I can't tonight,' she interrupted hurriedly. Heaven alone knew what time she would finish work tonight. Tomorrow, though, with Joel up in Scotland, should be much easier. 'I can make tomorrow if—'

Philip snapped up the alternative, asked again for her address, and when she had told him where she lived he, as busy as she, said he would look forward to tomorrow and rang off.

After that Chesnie was too busy to give thought to anything but the work she was involved with. She stayed late at her desk; so too did the man in the next room. At ten past seven she tidied her desk for the day, double-checked that Joel had all the information he would need for his trip, and went in to see him.

They spent another ten minutes finalising everything, then she said she was going home—and found she was looking into a pair of inscrutable sharp blue eyes.

He was unsmiling at first, but then relaxed to say quietly, 'You're turning out to be something of a treasure, Chesnie Cosgrove.'

Her heart gave the most peculiar bump, and she was so delighted by the compliment that she almost fell for his charm and smiled. But she wasn't forgetting his attitude earlier in the day, so she remained pleasant, but otherwise aloof, as—like any well-brought-up PA would—she wished him a pleasant trip and went home.

Strangely—or perhaps, she mused, it wasn't so strange— Joel Davenport was in her head very much that night. She could not remember ever being so annoyed with an employer before. Hector Browning didn't count; it was his father she had worked for.

Feeling unable to settle, Joel Davenport still in her head, she rang her sister at half past nine. 'I expected you to ring before this,' Nerissa said by way of apology. 'He rang, didn't he?'

'Did you have to tell him where I work?'

'What else could I do? You said not to give him your phone number. And anyway, I ran out of excuses. Where's he taking you?'

'I don't know. He's calling for me at—'

'Hah!' Nerissa cut in. 'You're going out with him!'

Chesnie had to laugh. 'Tomorrow,' she agreed, then chatted for another few minutes and rang off—to have Joel Davenport back in her head. He thought she was a treasure. She found she was smiling—and quickly cancelled that. Soft soap!

As anticipated, she was less busy on Thursday, and was extremely pleased that she seemed to coast through her work that day. True, there wasn't the same buzz about the office with Joel not there, but at least it looked as if she would be leaving on time that night. Which would suit her quite nicely. Time to go home, have a relaxing bath and get ready to go out with Philip Pomeroy.

At five past four she glanced at her watch, assessed the work she still had to do and knew for certain that she would be leaving at five. The best-laid plans...

At four-thirty her phone rang. 'Joel Davenport's office,' she answered pleasantly.

'Hello, Chesnie,' the man himself answered, and her insides went all kind of crumbly. Ridiculous, she told herself stoutly. 'I'm sorry to trouble you,' he began, not sounding sorry at all, 'but I've arranged an early meeting in London tomorrow. Do you think you can have some paperwork ready for me?'

'Of course,' she answered automatically, and had her notepad in hand. 'Fire away.'

She was getting writer's cramp before he was halfway finished. Was he joking? It would take her hours to complete this little lot! She almost stopped him then and there, to remind him that she had a date that night. But remembered in time how at her job interview he had asked her supposing she had a date but he needed her to accompany him at short notice. Without hesitation she'd indicated it would not be a problem—that she would change her plans for the evening. This wasn't accompanying him anywhere, but it amounted to the same thing.

'I haven't given you too much to do there, have I?' he asked, when he eventually came to an end.

'What are treasures for?' she found she had answered, before she could think about it.

'I knew I could rely on you,' he commented charmingly, and rang off.

Chesnie was busying herself making a start, collecting information together, before she realised that there was no way she could get everything sorted, no way she could type up reams and reams of confidential matter, *and* keep her date with Philip Pomeroy.

Her hand went to the phone, but before she could carry out her intention to put a call through to Symington Technology she had another thought. How about if she got all the paperwork already to hand checked over, then typed as much as she could of the new stuff before she went home? Then, with her computer installed at home in that apology for a second bedroom, she could work as late as she had to *after* her dinner with Philip. Brilliant, or what?

Having gone over the notion, Chesnie couldn't fault the idea. She'd have to get up early to have everything ready on Joel's desk for when he came in—she wished she knew what time that was—but couldn't see any problem. If this was what being a senior PA was all about, then she would prove she was very much up to the job.

She was glad to make herself comfortable in Philip Pomeroy's car on the way to the restaurant. It was the first chance she'd had to sit and relax since that half past four phone call. She had rushed from the office at five past six, laden with folders and stationery. She had taken the quickest of showers and had selected a short-sleeved, straight-skirted black dress. Although her wardrobe was not extensive it was of good quality. She had been ready and, anxious not to waste a minute, had been busy typing when the outer door buzzer had sounded, announcing the arrival of her escort.

The Linton, the restaurant Philip had chosen, was elegant, discreet, and, she didn't doubt, pricey. Chesnie found Philip Pomeroy a pleasant companion, too sophisticated to be obvious or pushy, and she began to relax more and more.

'I had no idea you worked for Joel Davenport,' Philip remarked as they began their meal. 'You can't have been at Yeatman Trading long or I'm sure I'd have heard.'

That surprised her. Then she wondered if it should have. Being a business rival, would Joel know the name of Philip's PA? Very probably he did, she mused.

'I've worked for Joel for almost two months now,' she saw no harm in admitting.

'You changed jobs around the same time you moved into your new flat,' Philip documented. 'How do you find working for Davenport? Is he—?'

'Hmm, I'm sorry, Philip, would you mind very much if neither of us talked about our work?'

He stared at her, plainly liked what he saw, and agreed. 'It's a pact. Business if off the agenda. But—' he smiled '—you can tell Davenport from me that he's a lucky devil, able to look at you every day. Now, tell me how you're settling in to your new flat?'

During their second course Chesnie learned that Philip had been married and divorced. That didn't worry her— who hadn't? She was growing to like him very much, even though she knew that it would never be more than that. He was amusing, and had just said something that made her laugh when, glancing from him, laughter still on her curving lips, she was startled to find she was looking into the steel-blue eyes of someone several tables away. The glint in those eyes warned her she was in trouble over something.

With a coolness she was suddenly far from feeling

Chesnie turned back to her dinner companion. She offered some light comment, she knew not what, her mind busy with the fact that Joel Davenport had flown back from Scotland and all too plainly, if her answers at the job interview meant anything, fully expected her to still be slaving away at the office.

It annoyed her that he should think she had fallen down on the job. And that annoyance caused her to smile more, perhaps laugh a little more, at Philip's amusingly light conversation than she would otherwise.

At any rate Philip seemed pleased, and she didn't give a button what Davenport thought. She knew what he didn't—that she was going home to do his work so he should have it on his desk for eight in the morning. So he could go and take a running jump.

'More coffee?' Philip asked.

'No, thank you,' she refused pleasantly. 'It's been a super evening, but…'

'But you're a working girl?'

'Something like that,' she answered with a smile, and smiled again when, having to pass Davenport's table—curse it—Philip civilly paused to say hello.

'Pomeroy,' Joel acknowledged, getting to his feet. 'Chesnie.' He included her, and introduced his sultry, if terrific-looking companion. 'Do you know Imogen?'

Brief introductions followed, where Joel did not mention that Chesnie was his PA and that he was saving a few short and sharp words for her. After the way she slaved for him! Let him try! Then she and Philip were moving on.

Philip came to the outer door of her apartment building with her. 'I hope you're going to allow me to see you again, Chesnie?' he asked.

She liked him, he was good company—and she had an idea it annoyed Joel Davenport that she went out with the opposition. 'I'd like that,' she answered. But, thinking he might have this coming Saturday in mind, added, 'I'll give you my phone number. Perhaps next week some time?'

'I'll look forward to it,' he said, and when he had her phone number he leaned forward. Though, perhaps sensing her instant withdrawal, he satisfied himself to kiss her cheek, and stood back to wait while she went indoors.

Despite the fact that her home had been cobbled together with pieces of furniture given to her by her parents, grand-parents and her sisters, and the few additions she had con-tributed herself, Chesnie had to admit everything blended in well to give her apartment a very homely feel.

But there was no time to make herself comfortable in it now. Time only to rinse her hands and head for that tiny second bedroom now laughingly called a study.

She had been at work for forty-five minutes when some-one rang the outer buzzer. Philip? Why would he come back? She left her work and went into her small hall to take up the telephone that was connected to the outer front door.

'Who is it?' she enquired, and felt faintly staggered at the reply she received.

'Davenport,' he informed her crisply.

Davenport! Surely he hadn't left the lovely Imogen to have those few short and sharp words with his PA that had been brewing? At this hour? She didn't believe it—though he wasn't sounding too affable.

'You'd better come up!' she replied, equally crisply, while wondering—had she done anything that could be called grounds for dismissal? She didn't think so, and surely Joel Davenport wouldn't call at her home to sack her! Or would he?

She stayed in the hall to wait the minute or so it would take him to reach her door, and mentally braced herself for whatever he had called to see her about. At his first ring she had the door open. For several seconds, like warring adversaries, they stood coldly eyeing each other. He was the first to speak.

'You're still dressed!' he stated hostilely, his glance go-ing over her black dress, drawn for a second to the delicate contours of her cleavage, which had never before been on view.

Feeling very much like holding her hands protectively in front of her bosom, Chesnie instead turned from him. 'Come in,' she invited, and led the way into her sitting room, realising that it would have been just the same to him if she had gone to bed—he would still have rung her apartment buzzer.

In her sitting room she turned to face him. But before she could ask him why he had called, *he* was telling *her*, 'You knew I needed that paperwork for the morning!' Clearly he had stopped by the office from the airport and discovered that the paperwork he'd ordered wasn't locked away in his drawer. 'Yet you deliberately—' He began to sort her out. But she'd had enough before he started.

'I'm glad you called,' she cut in calmly, inwardly boiling. 'There are one or two queries I need your help with. If you're not too tired after your busy day, I wonder if you'd help me?' He was looking at her with narrowed eyes, as if wondering what her game was. Oh, joy; oh, bliss. 'Have you a moment to come to my study?' Study? Pretentious or what? 'I'm working on your paperwork now.'

There was a definite glint in his eyes now, she saw. He had called looking for a fight. She had disarmed him—and he didn't like it. Tough.

Whether he was impressed or not that she'd had no intention of letting him down, she had no idea. But he followed her to her 'study', where she had already printed off some of the matter she had typed.

Swiftly he dealt with the queries which she had been going to make a note of, but from the unsmiling look of him she suspected he didn't care at all to have his cause for righteous anger taken away from him, and was still looking for a fight.

'Naturally, I intend to have everything completed and on

your desk by eight in the morning.' She nicely rubbed it in.

A hostile look was the thanks she received for her trouble. She was almost purring as they left her workroom and she accompanied him out to the hall. He soon put an end to any lofty feelings, however.

Joel Davenport had his hand on the door latch when he looked down on her from his superior height, paused, and then commented shortly, 'After our discussion yesterday, I hardly expected you to be out with Pomeroy tonight!'

What discussion was that? Her memory of it was that Joel had enlightened her to the fact that Philip Pomeroy was head of the opposition. And she felt incensed again that Davenport, for a second time, felt he had to remind her of the confidentiality of her position!

'Do you honestly believe that Philip would have telephoned me at the office and told you who he was if he was after sensitive information from me?' she flared. And, her cool image suddenly in tatters around her, 'Do you honestly think, when I've worked for you for almost two months now, that I would part with any information, confidential or otherwise?' she erupted—and came the closest yet to setting about him when, infuriatingly, he stared at her, seemed again to enjoy seeing her lose her cool front, and then had the sheer audacity—to smile!

'It seems a shame that, because of pressure of work, you sent him from your first date without even a goodnight kiss,' he commented charmingly.

Oh, to kick his shin! Chesnie strove hard for control. 'It rather looks as if you're going to bed kissless too,' she answered sweetly—and was on the receiving end of a look that very clearly stated *'Fat chance'*. Though he made no comment with regard to whether the delectable Imogen was waiting for him somewhere.

Instead, he opened the door, and was on his way out when he bade her silkily, 'Don't work too late.'

Chesnie glared at his departing back. Pig!

CHAPTER THREE

OVER the month that followed Chesnie grew more and more comfortable with her job, and now found the work well within her capabilities. It was hard work, many late evenings, and once, when there had been a big boardroom pow-wow, she had worked a whole weekend. But she loved it, thrived on it, and couldn't think of ever doing anything else. It was as though she had found her niche in life, as though working for Joel was what she was meant to be doing.

Ever since that night when he had called at her flat and found, contrary to his expectations, that she had not fallen down on the job and that his paperwork would be ready for him for the next day, as required, they had settled down to a good, mutually respectful, harmonious working relationship.

Since that night too, the night she had given Philip Pomeroy her home number, Philip had made frequent use of it—but had not again telephoned her at her office. She sometimes went out with him, but he knew by then—or she hoped he did—that she was only interested in being friends. True, he always kissed her cheek on parting—but friends did that sort of thing. She was seeing Philip again tomorrow evening.

But Philip Pomeroy was far from her thoughts that Friday morning when the phone on her desk suddenly called for attention. 'Joel Davenport's office,' she answered automatically.

'That has to be the delightful Chesnie,' said a mature voice she took a moment or two to place.

'Magnus!' she exclaimed, a smile in her voice. 'I'm

afraid Joel's out for the rest of the morning, and part of this afternoon. Did you want him for anything in particular? Or is there something I can help you with?'

'I haven't had a chat to you in a long while,' he replied.

That was true. It must be all of five, maybe six weeks since she'd taken Joel's father to lunch. 'How are you?' she asked, sensing he wanted to chat a little.

Several seconds of silence met her enquiry, then, his voice sounding frail and elderly all of a sudden, he answered at last. 'To tell you the truth, Chesnie, there have been days when I've felt better.'

'You're unwell?' she questioned, starting to feel worried. From his earlier bright tone—clearly a front—he had gone to sound alarmingly shaky.

'I'll—be all right,' he replied bravely.

That wasn't good enough. 'Have you seen a doctor?' she asked, not feeling at all as calm as she was pretending to be.

'I'll be all right,' he repeated, which she took to mean that he hadn't.

'Do you think you should?'

'I'll think about it,' he said, which she just knew meant he had no intention of seeing a doctor.

'Do you have anybody with you?' she asked.

'Who wants to keep company with an old codger like me?' he answered, plainly not feeling his best.

Chesnie chatted to him for about another five minutes, trying to find out what the exact trouble was. He wasn't saying. She gave up when she realised it might be something he was a little embarrassed about.

She was still feeling worried when Magnus rang off. It could be something; it could be nothing. She knew where she could contact Joel—but what if it was nothing? What would Joel do, anyway? Leave his meeting to go and check on his father? From what she'd gleaned, Joel wasn't over-struck on his father anyhow.

For the next half-hour thoughts of Magnus Davenport

being unwell and on his own chewed at her. It was a quarter to one when she couldn't stand it any longer. She liked him. She decided to contact the switchboard, ask them to take messages for her and go for an early lunch. She had his card somewhere—she'd drive over to see him.

It took her three quarters of an hour to get to Magnus Davenport's address, and, having pulled up at the very nice-looking house, Chesnie hoped he would be fit enough to come to the door. It might be that he hadn't moved from where he'd been sitting when he had telephoned her.

She was, she discovered, wrong in a lot of her assumptions. Her ring at the doorbell was answered immediately, and, standing there smiling, Magnus Davenport looked as sprightly as ever.

She opened her mouth—he spoke first. 'I thought you'd never get here!' he exclaimed cheerfully.

He had been expecting her? 'You're—not ill?' she questioned. He looked and sounded in the best of health!

'I'm lonely,' he answered.

And Chesnie just stared at him. There was *nothing* wrong with him, and she was going to have to work late tonight to make up for her earlier lack of concentration and the time she'd taken out when she should have been working. 'You want me to take you to lunch?' she guessed—he was dressed as smart as new paint.

'I've had a few winners lately.' He grinned. 'I'll pay.'

She wanted to be cross with him—he had conned her into driving to see him. But how could she be cross? He was grinning like a mischievous schoolboy, and had admitted to being lonely.

He was his usual indiscreet chatty self over lunch, with tales that most often began with, 'When Dorothea threw me out...' This way Chesnie learned he had been on his uppers with nowhere to go when Joel had come to the rescue and had bought him his house. Joel, it seemed, also gave him a monthly allowance.

'I'd rather have had a lump sum, but Joel said I'd be

bound to spend it all in one go on the gee-gees. He knows me too well,' Magnus complained wryly. 'Arlene Yeatman's still after him, I suppose?'

Arlene Enderby, née Yeatman. 'I've no idea.'

'She was after him even before she ditched her husband and got her divorce. She—'

'I don't think you should tell me...'

'Not you as well!' He laughed. 'Dorothea always used to accuse me of being worse than some gossipy old washerwoman.'

Chesnie smiled a gentle smile. 'You still care for her, don't you?'

'Dorothea? Adore the old battleaxe,' he admitted, and Chesnie's smile turned into a laugh. He really was incorrigible.

She was very late getting back to her office. It had gone three when she hurried in— Lord knew what time she'd be working until that night. And Joel was back, the door between the two offices open.

First dropping her bag down on her desk, she went in to see him. 'Sorry I'm late,' she apologised, out of courtesy. 'I hope you didn't need me for anything?'

'Been shopping?' he enquired mildly, his glance going over her sage-green short-jacketed suit, its just-above-the-knee skirt showing the long, slender length of her legs and trim ankles.

'I've been out to lunch,' she answered.

'The time you put in you're entitled to more than an extended lunch,' he replied, and she knew she was right; their working relationship really was harmonious. Or she'd thought she was right, until all at once his relaxed manner vanished and, 'Who with?' he demanded.

Slightly shaken by his change in attitude, it took all her will-power to stay looking calm. 'As it happens, I had lunch with your father,' she replied coolly—she had intended to tell him anyway, and to mention his father's loneliness at the same time.

'The devil you did! He came here, conning you—'

'He rang,' she cut in, starting to get cross and having great difficulty in hiding it. 'I got the impression that Magnus wasn't feeling well. You weren't here, and I didn't want to disturb your meeting if—'

'You would have interrupted my meeting on account of that cunning old fox spinning you some yarn?' he queried, looking astounded.

Chesnie, realising from that comment that Joel knew his father only too well, ignored Joel's look of astonishment, though didn't feel too clever at how easily she had been taken in.

'He didn't actually say he was ill,' she confessed, recalling that Magnus had merely said that there were days when he had felt better.

'But he alarmed you sufficiently for you to decide that rather than contact me—for which I thank you,' he inserted sarcastically, not looking in the least grateful, 'you'd meet him for lunch.'

'I didn't plan it at all. I just—got worried. So in the end I drove over to see him.'

'You went to his house?' Hostility was rife. 'How did you know where he lived?'

What *was* this? 'He gave me his card so I could ring him—the last time I had lunch with him.'

'He wanted you to call him?'

If Joel was getting angry, Chesnie was getting furious. 'Only if I wanted to go to the races with him, which I didn't. Anyway—'

'Anyway, you went over to his home and found he wasn't at all unwell, but merely wanted to dupe you out of another lunch.'

'He paid!' she erupted, no longer able to hold it in. 'And don't talk about him like that!' she snapped, her control flying. She was too furious to care that his eyebrows shot up in amazement. 'He's your father,' she stormed on. 'And he's lonely, and—'

'And no doubt you cheered him up!' Joel snarled, getting angrily to his feet, not at all enamoured of her telling him what not to do, nor her nerve in taking it upon herself to defend *his* father.

'What are you implying?' she flew, angry sparks flashing in her furious green eyes.

'You tell me! What's going on?' he demanded, coming round to where she stood.

'Don't *you* start!' she exploded, hurling the words at him, feeling within an ace of hitting him. She strove desperately for control. No man had ever riled her so! Somehow, though, she managed to harness her fury, sufficient anyway to inform Joel Davenport crisply, 'Just as I had no intention of becoming Hector Browning's stepmother, I've no intention of becoming your stepmother either!'

She saw his jaw clench, but recognised that he seemed to have got to grips with his anger too. Though she wasn't feeling in any way friendly to him when, 'Close the door on your way out,' he instructed her coldly.

Chesnie marched back to her own office, her control hanging on sufficiently that she didn't give in to her urge to slam the door hard enough behind her to make the fixtures and fittings rattle. It would not have taken much for her to pick up her bag and to keep on walking. She had to admit she felt very much like doing just that.

But her control held. Swine of a man—what had happened to 'harmonious'? She slaved for him! He didn't deserve her! How on earth had Barbara Platt put up with him? In the absence of slamming the door, Chesnie slammed into her work, mutinying angrily against the man she had the misfortune to work for.

She was still inwardly raging against him when she had work ready that required his signature. He could jolly well come and get it! But her professionalism chose that moment to trip her up.

She got to her feet, collected everything together in a folder and, opening the connecting door, went smartly into the other office. He was seated behind his desk. If he looked up from what he was absorbed with she didn't notice—she wasn't looking at him. She spotted a clear space on his desk, placed the folder down and, without comment, went smartly out again, closing the door behind her.

Quite when during the next sixty minutes Chesnie began to see things from Joel's angle, she didn't know. She didn't want to see things from his point of view, she knew that; she wanted to stay furious with him. How dared he ask 'What's going on?' just as though she was some harpy with designs on his father?

Against that, though, who did she think she was, defending his father to him? Joel had known his father for longer, and knew him far better than she. He probably loved him, though he'd probably never admit to it. Knowing his father for the con-merchant he undoubtedly was hadn't stopped Joel from seeing to it that his father had a roof over his head and money in his pocket.

That was no reason for him to speak to her the way he had, though, she fumed in another moment of rebellion. But she knew that her rebellion was not as strong as it had been.

It was a little after six when Joel came through to her office with the folder she had placed on his desk. She thought he would just put it down and leave. But he didn't, and the mere fact of him holding on to it made her look up.

He was unsmiling, but he was no longer angry, she saw. And as he held out his right hand to shake hands she realised he had cooled down and was making a gesture of truce.

'I can't go home wondering if I'm still going to have a PA come Monday,' he said quietly, every bit as if he was aware she had come close to walking out earlier.

Selfish devil! All he cared about was his work! 'We were both in the wrong,' she felt fair-minded enough to reply, while at the same time wondering what *else* should he care about, for goodness' sake? Her? Don't be ridiculous. 'But since you apologise so nicely…' She extended her right hand—and felt an undeniable thrill when Joel took it in his firm grip. Grief! Their furious spat must have unhinged her!

'Have you much more to do?' Joel asked, letting go her hand.

She did a rough calculation. 'I should be through about seven,' she calculated.

'Same here. I'll take you for a spot of dinner, if you like.'

She'd had better-phrased offers. 'I had a big lunch,' she refused. 'Thank you all the same.'

Chesnie had known many emotions that day, but as she later drove home she realised she was feeling almost tearful—and could only put that down to the fact that, having felt more furious that day than at any time in her life, she was so very glad that Joel had been big enough to put an end to hostilities. She must be feeling tearful out of relief that they had made it up.

Philip took her to a symphony concert on Saturday. It was enjoyable, but the evening took a quite alarming turn when, after pulling up outside her apartment building, Philip said that he wanted to have a talk with her about something.

He sounded serious and, while she hadn't a clue what he wanted to talk to her about, she liked him too well to suggest he tell her in the car what he obviously thought was important.

'Would you like to chat over coffee?' she offered.

She was in her small kitchen making coffee, and wondered, for all they had agreed on their first date not to talk business, if he was perhaps bursting with news of some coup or other that Symington Technology had just pulled off.

Hearing a sound behind her, she turned and saw that Philip had just come into the kitchen. She was just about to make some laughing comment to the effect that the kitchen wasn't big enough for two when, to her utter consternation, Philip exclaimed, 'You're driving me mad, Chesnie!' She stared at him in astonishment. 'I'm in love with you, yet I'm not allowed to touch you, to come near you. I want to marry you, but...'

'Philip—don't!' she cried in total dismay.

'You're shutting me out again!' he protested.

'Philip, I...' she said helplessly, all thought of coffee forgotten.

'I'm sorry. I'm not doing this very well. I hadn't meant to blurt it out like that. At my age you'd think I'd have more control.'

She was starting to feel claustrophobic. The kitchen was small, and Philip was blocking the doorway. 'Let's go and sit down,' she suggested, and was relieved when, like a lamb, he moved to let her out. But in the sitting room Chesnie was stumped to know what to say. 'I'm sorry,' she in turn apologised, 'I had no idea I'd encouraged you to think...'

'That's just it. You haven't given me any encouragement at all. I would dearly love to hold you close, but I know you'd never consent to go out with me again if I attempted it.'

She was starting to think it would perhaps be better if she didn't go out with him again anyway. But he seemed to read her mind and, over the next ten minutes, implored her not to break with him and to let him see her again. He looked so strained, so anguished suddenly, that she found she could not do what her every instinct told her to do.

'I want to marry you, that's irrefutable, but promise to see me again and I'll promise not to mention it again until I see some sign that you want me to,' he urged. 'It wouldn't hurt you. *I'd* never hurt you, Chesnie—and it's not as if you're in love with anybody else.'

Why in creation a picture of Joel Davenport giving her one of his rare smiles should come into her mind's eye, she had no idea. 'No,' she agreed, 'I'm not in love with anybody else.'

'There you are, then.' He smiled winningly. 'Say you'll have dinner with me next Saturday, no hard feelings. Then I can ask you what I meant to ask you before the sight of you looking so beautiful in the kitchen turned my insides to jelly and my brain to mush.'

Good heavens! She made a mental note to stay out of the kitchen whenever Philip was near. 'That wasn't it?' she questioned. 'Er—that—your...'

'My proposal? No. I knew the time wasn't right. It doesn't alter what I feel, what I want—I just got my timing all wrong.' He looked at her for long moments, then collected himself to state, 'My long-suffering PA has today told me she's had enough. I wanted to ask you if you fancied coming to work for me?'

She hadn't got over her first surprise yet, and here he was issuing another one. 'I don't think...' she began.

'You can name your own salary,' he jumped in quickly. 'Any package you want is yours. You—'

'You're chancing it!' She had to smile. 'You don't know if I'm any good at my job or not.'

'Davenport wouldn't keep you on for a minute if you weren't. Besides, I've heard that you're close to being brilliant at the work you do.'

Chesnie wasn't so sure she liked the sound of that. When all was said and done the firm Philip was head of was still the opposition. Did Symington Technology have a spy in the camp of Yeatman Trading? She realised that it was a fact of life that staff were invariably constantly on the move. It wouldn't be a highly confidential matter for some one-time Yeatman employee on transfer to a similar company to comment that Joel Davenport's new PA was proving up to the job.

Having declined Philip's job offer, Chesnie was still feeling a little shaken by his surprising marriage proposal the next morning when her mother telephoned—mainly, it seemed, to give her a catalogue of her father's wrongdoings. Chesnie knew that her mother would not be entirely blameless—the plain fact was that her parents didn't see eye-to-eye on *anything*. Long experience had taught Chesnie not to take sides, but at the end of that phone call she felt emotionally drained.

Marriage! Who wanted it? Marriage—you could keep it as far as she was concerned. One way and another she was having quite an emotional time of it. It had started with her argument with Joel on Friday and gone on to Philip last night, her mother just now—if any of her sisters phoned to complain about their lot, she'd tell them to ring some other time.

Monday started the busiest week she had ever known. Joel spared neither himself nor her. The morning flew by. She had a sandwich at her desk at lunchtime.

Knowing that there was a full board meeting at two, Chesnie went into Joel's office at a quarter to the hour and was taken aback to see Arlene Enderby, sitting cosily with Joel at his desk, her tinkly laugh trilling out at something he had just said.

For no reason it irked Chesnie that Arlene Enderby had come in through the other door to see Joel. But, masking her feelings, Chesnie handed Joel the figures he required and went back to her desk, wondering what on earth was the matter with her? If any of the other directors wished to see Joel they often used that self-same door.

Joel was back from his meeting at four. He called her in to his office. 'A few notes,' he said, and proceeded with a list so long she felt like checking the dictionary meaning of the word 'few'. Nor had he finished when, notes taken, he informed her, 'We're in Glasgow tomorrow.' We? Him and Arlene? Chesnie felt her stomach muscles cramp up. 'Book accommodation for one night,' he went on, 'and an early flight.' And while Chesnie, to her own amazement, was fiercely determined he and laughing-girl would be having separate rooms, he looked up to enquire, 'You do know the way to the airport?'

She almost exclaimed *Me?* but in time remembered her

cool image. 'Of course,' she lied. *She* was going to Scotland with him! She was going on her first trip with him!

Joel relaxed for a moment to comment dryly, 'I trust you won't have to break a theatre date.'

Her lips twitched. She controlled herself, but, looking at him, saw that his gaze was on her mouth, and knew that he had noticed she had almost lost her cool front for a moment then.

When Chesnie fell into bed that night she knew she was going to sleep soundly. She was exhausted. Work had been non-stop that day, and she only hoped she had got everything right. She had contacted the hotel Joel usually used and, bearing in mind Barbara Platt had told her that he did not hold with the antiquated nonsense of his PA being on a separate floor— 'In other words if he wants to contact you around midnight with some query or work to be done you'll be near at hand.' —Chesnie had booked their accommodation on the same floor. Because she couldn't see the point of her going if she was not intending to work, she booked a suite of rooms with a computer facility for him, and a room for herself.

The only respite the next day was during the seventy-five-minute flight. But even then Joel spent time instructing her and filling her in on the meeting she was attending with him.

A car was there waiting for them at Glasgow airport, and whisked them off to their hotel. Since she had thought to freshen up at the airport, while waiting the short while for their overnight bags to arrive, it was just a matter of taking their luggage and the laptop Chesnie had decided to bring at the last moment up to their hotel rooms, and going straight out again to their first meeting.

Joel was indefatigable; she'd give him that. Even in the late afternoon he was assimilating in moments complicated matter that had her struggling. By the skin of her teeth she managed to keep up, but she wasn't sorry when at six-fifteen the last of their meetings that day wound down and Joel said they'd go back to their hotel.

Chesnie had no doubt that she had not finished for the day, but was pleasantly surprised when, having collected their keys, ridden up in the lift and stepped out at their floor, Joel suggested, 'See you in the bar for a drink before dinner? Around seven?'

'Good idea,' she agreed, and left him, no longer wondering why businessmen—or any true worker, for that matter—liked a pick-me-up at the end of a hard and strenuous day. She knew just how they felt.

She had packed a crease-resistant casual trouser suit and was pleased she had. She was glad to get out of her 'office' clothes, take a shower and get dressed again in something casual.

Chesnie applied the small amount of make-up she normally wore, brushed her shoulder-length red-blonde hair, and at a few minutes after seven left her room and went down to the hotel's bar. She admitted to herself that, for someone who had earlier been very much feeling the effects of a non-stop working day, she was now feeling a little excited. How strange!

Joel was already in the bar. He was nursing a Scotch, but was on his feet when he saw her, and she saw his glance flick over her long-legged trouser-clad form. 'What are you having?' he enquired pleasantly.

She asked for a gin and tonic but, mindful that he would probably want to put in a few hours of work after dinner, decided one gin and tonic would be sufficient alcohol to 'pick-her-up'.

Joel was good company away from the office, she discovered, chatting lightly and easily away, his manner remaining pleasant and just as easy when they went into dinner.

They were into the main course of their meal when, having briefly discussed a play they had both seen, Joel paused, studied her, and then enquired casually, 'Still seeing Pomeroy?'

Chesnie studied Joel in return, trying to gauge from his equally casual expression what, if anything, lay behind his question. 'Occasionally,' she replied steadily, her insides starting to knot up, hoping they weren't going to have a fight in a public dining room.

Blue eyes fixed on her green eyes. 'How is he?' he asked civilly.

As if he cared! 'We have a pact never to discuss business,' she replied to the question she was certain he was asking.

'A pact!' His look was sardonic. '*That* occasionally?'

Oh, stuff it! Somehow Chesnie managed to stay looking outwardly calm, admitting that to have such a pact with a man she saw only 'occasionally' did sound a bit odd. 'That confidential,' she replied, her hackles starting to rise as she recalled Joel's icy manner that day Philip had phoned her at the office.

'I don't doubt it,' Joel replied pleasantly, and at that vote of faith Chesnie's raised hackles disappeared. She even smiled, a natural and—for the moment—unguarded smile. It was a mistake. She saw his glance go to her mouth. Indeed, he was still surveying its pleasing curve when, clearly not done with the subject of Philip Pomeroy yet, Joel abruptly left his contemplation of her mouth and, looking straight into her eyes, bluntly asked, 'So what package did he try to tempt you with?'

'Package?' she questioned, for the moment not with him.

'Don't tell me he didn't come head-hunting!'

'Head-hunting!' she exclaimed, catching up fast. 'I'm that good?'

'You're prevaricating!' he accused toughly.

'Why on earth would I want to leave you?' she retaliated, and could have sworn she saw a hint of a twitch on his superb bottom lip. Superb! Yoiks!

Any notion she might have nursed that he had found her

answer a touch humorous was proved erroneous, however, when, as bluntly as before, he stated, 'So you turned him down.' But, his eyes suddenly alert, he leaned back in his chair and questioned tautly, 'A job wasn't all this man you see only "occasionally" offered, was it?'

Honestly! She worked for this man; he didn't own her! Stubbornly Chesnie looked back at him—as if she'd say! She put down her knife and fork and smiled her guarded smile. 'That pie was delicious.'

'So you turned down that proposal too?'

She stared at him, wondering how she could like this tenacious man and yet, at the same time, would be quite happy to punch him on the nose. 'Look,' she said on a hiss of sound, 'I don't know how we got onto the subject of Philip Pomeroy—' they had been enjoying a perfectly pleasant evening up until then—well, at least she had '—but if your questioning is on account of some notion you have that I may give up my job at a moment's notice— and I'm sure Eileen Gray or any one of the other PAs would fill in quite adequately until you could get someone else—then I'll tell you what I told Philip. I have no intention of leaving Yeatman Trading.' She stared forthrightly into a pair of unflinching sharp blue eyes. 'Unless I'm pushed,' she added. 'And I'd remind you of what I said at interview—that I am not, repeat not, remotely interested in marriage!' There! It had been quite a speech, and had been spurred on by a growing niggle of annoyance, but she didn't regret a word of it.

That was, she hadn't thought she did until Joel Davenport's brow went up and, 'Marriage!' he exclaimed. 'Pomeroy offered you marriage?'

'What the Dickens did you think he'd proposed?' She was starting to get really angry, and was glad the dining room was spacious and that their table seemed to be a cosy one, not too close to other diners.

Joel looked at her—looked at her as if really seeing her. 'Oh, Chesnie Cosgrove,' he answered, a smile coming to his wonderful mouth. 'Looking at you, half a dozen offers spring to mind.' She blinked. Surely he wasn't being personal? 'Not for myself, of course,' he hastened to assure her. 'I'm more than happy with the relationship we have— our working relationship.'

At that point the waiter came to clear the used dishes away and returned with the pudding menu. And Joel Davenport went back to being a pleasant host and boss, and spoke of anything that came to mind other than business.

But it ferreted away at Chesnie that she had revealed what she considered to be personal to Philip. She hadn't meant to, she had just let her guard slip for once, and Joel now knew that the proposal Philip had made was one of marriage.

She and Joel were standing waiting for the lift when Chesnie knew that she wouldn't be able to go to bed until she had said something. She turned to the tall man by her side, saw that he was looking down at her, that she had his attention, and the words just came bursting from her. 'I didn't mean to say—about Philip.' Joel looked as though he might laugh. 'I wish I hadn't,' she went on. He had to know she was serious. 'It was unfair to him. It's—'

'What a truly nice person you are,' Joel cut in. She stared at him—he was good at soft soap. Was this some more of it? 'Nice, sensitive—and I promise I'll respect your confidences.'

Whether it was flattery or not, she knew she could believe him. 'Thank you, Joel,' she said quietly, and went into the lift with him.

They had the lift to themselves, and he had pressed the button to their floor when he turned to her to ask, 'What is it exactly you have against marriage?'

'Apart from the divorce statistics, you mean? Where would you like me to start?'

'You've never been married?' he asked abruptly.

'No!' she replied, more sharply than she'd meant to.

'I've seen enough of other people's marriages to know I don't need it.'

'In your own family?' he guessed.

She knew his parents were divorced, so deemed it a fair question. 'I have three sisters—their marriages range from rocky, shattered to divorced. Though the divorced one did try again.' She broke off jerkily. 'I shouldn't be telling you this.'

'Yes, you should,' he contradicted. 'Besides, I asked you. How's the remarriage going?' Chesnie decided she didn't want to tell him anything more. What went on between Nerissa and Stephen was private. To his credit, Joel didn't press her for a reply to that question, but as the lift doors opened he had not yet done with his questions. 'How about your parents' marriage?' he enquired. 'Still surviving?'

'It's been hanging by a thread for years,' she found she had replied, before she knew it. And, in a bid to get the conversation on a work-oriented course, quite off the top of her head invited, 'You have my room number if you need me during the night.' She would have thought no more about it had not Joel stopped dead and stared at her. She stopped too, and looked at him. Then suddenly she went scarlet. 'Work!' she said hurriedly. 'If—if you want me to work...' She felt hot all over.

'You're blushing,' Joel remarked. 'Well, well, my cool Miss Cosgrove.'

'Goodnight!' she said abruptly, and marched off to her room. Pig! she fumed. Pig!

Inside her room, she strove to get herself together. It wasn't her fault; she'd thought he might want her to work late into the night. As he hadn't mentioned anything about work, it was only natural that she should have offered, made herself available...

Oh, hang it. What was it about the man? She couldn't understand it, him either, or even her own self. Some things—family things, Philip things, confidences such as those—were sacrosanct. Wild horses, she would have said, prior to this evening, would not have dragged from her what she had just told Joel Davenport about her personal life.

So what was it about him that had seen her opening up the way she had? She had never opened up to anyone else that way before. True, she had every faith that what she'd said would go no further. But if Joel could keep such matters to himself, why in the world hadn't she been able to do the same?

She was forced to admit that the answer to that was simply that she didn't know why. But what she *did* know, as she considered how easily Joel was able to get under her carefully built up guard—be it by annoying her, making her angry, making her furious, and now even making her blush—was that no man she had ever met had his power to so effortlessly shatter her equilibrium.

CHAPTER FOUR

THEY arrived back in London early the next afternoon. While Joel had gone to another meeting Chesnie had spent the morning beavering away on the previous day's notes. She still hadn't finished when Joel had returned to the hotel, but after a snatched meal they'd gone straight to the airport and on to the office.

The London office was buzzing, as usual, and there didn't seem a minute to spare. Chesnie at last caught up with her work, and the previous day's messages—though if she worked hard, she just had to admire the amount of work Joel got through. No sooner had he caught up on his backlog than he was off to an 'in-house' meeting. He returned to instruct her to set up another meeting, for nine the following morning, and stayed at his desk to make some phone calls.

At half past six Vernon Gillespie and Russell Yeatman, two of the directors whom Chesnie knew were in favour of Joel taking over the chairmanship, stopped by Joel's office briefly before the three of them went off to a conference.

Chesnie, knowing that the conference Joel was attending would go on for hours, worked until seven. She hoped they would have some kind of refreshment at the conference. Joel had barely eaten... Abruptly she brought herself up short. He was a grown man, for goodness' sake! Well able to look after himself and find himself something to eat.

Chesnie went home certain that her concern for Joel was nothing more than a natural interest anyone would have when they witnessed at first hand the sort of day Joel put in.

That feeling of concern was still with her, however, when she changed from her smart business suit. She usually showered last thing at night, but, feeling in need of revitalising, she took a shower, donned jeans and a tee shirt—and her concern over Joel was still there. It remained with her when, feeling too tired to want to cook properly, she made herself some cheese on toast. Somehow she couldn't stop thinking about Joel.

By ten she was half decided to go to bed. She admitted she felt tired enough to sleep the clock round—yet at the same time she felt restless, unable to settle. She decided instead to have a tidy round.

Her flat was usually fairly neat and tidy, and was soon dealt with. She was again considering going to bed when, to her surprise, her telephone rang. She answered on the second ring.

'Good, you're still up!' Joel said. Her heart gave a most unexpected flutter, and even as she wondered why Joel would phone at this hour she found she was smiling. Though not for long when, abruptly, and not very pleasantly, 'Are you alone?' he fired.

Chesnie took a steadying breath. 'Good evening, Joel,' she replied sweetly, her ultra-pleasantness making up for his lack of it. 'How did your conference go?'

'Funny you should ask,' he answered, sudden good humour pushing away any sign of aggressiveness. 'I've just come away now. Um—I could really do with some paperwork for that meeting tomorrow.'

'Your nine o'clock meeting?' she enquired carefully, not thrilled at the idea of getting dressed in her business suit at this time of night and driving to the offices of Yeatman Trading. For preference she'd rather get up before dawn cracked and get to the office around five.

'You've remembered,' he flattered.

'Cut the flannel!' she retorted, quite without thinking, and added, 'Sir,' for the hell of it. 'It would take me half an hour to three-quarters to get to the office tonight. But I could—'

'I wouldn't dream of asking you to turn out of your cosy apartment at this time of night,' Joel cut her off.

'You—wouldn't?' she questioned slowly, not believing it for a second—and was staggered by his answer.

'I'm outside your place now,' he said matter-of-factly. He was outside now! On his mobile phone! But there was no time for her to think further because he was going on succinctly, 'And you've got a computer…'

She hadn't a scrap of make-up on, and looked down at her jeans—clean, neat—but she didn't want to be seen by him looking anything but her best. Ridiculous! she scoffed the moment the thought was born. 'Ring the buzzer; I'll let you up,' she said in her best PA voice.

Joel rang off and she had time just to run a comb through her hair, check her appearance—then the buzzer sounded. She pressed the button to unlock the front door and in no time was opening her door to the man she worked for.

'Come in,' she invited, and he stepped into her hall.

She closed the door, but before she could follow through her intention to lead him straight to her 'study' she was arrested by the way he was looking at her. 'Lovely.' The word seemed to escape him. 'You know you're lovely.'

Her throat went suddenly dry. He thought her lovely— without a scrap of make-up, he thought her lovely! 'If you say so,' she somehow managed lightly. 'I wouldn't dream of arguing.' His glance went from her face to flick over her shapely figure and she was very much aware that this was the first time he had seen her in casual attire. 'Have you eaten?' she asked in a rush, having not meant to ask anything of the sort.

'Of course,' he answered, 'at lunchtime.'

He hadn't eaten since lunch! 'How does cheese on toast sound?' she offered, reflecting that fifteen minutes either way would make no difference to the time they finished work.

'A feast,' he accepted, and she led the way to the sitting room.

He had been up early that morning, as had she, but she'd had time to rest between now and then—and his day wasn't over yet. She left him seated on her sofa, hoping that perhaps he might relax for five minutes while she was in the kitchen, but he was already delving into his briefcase.

While he demolished cheese on toast and drank a couple of cups of coffee Joel talked her through the business of the next few hours. It was eleven o'clock by the time Chesnie had her computer turned on. While she worked Joel was busy with more work of his own, but was on hand for queries—the hours just flew.

At three minutes past two Chesnie switched off her computer. 'That's the lot,' she said, getting up and putting all the paperwork together. Only then did she allow herself to acknowledge how tired she felt. But, aside from the fact she was paid a whale of a salary, Joel was good to work for, stimulating to work for—but now he must be feeling as drained as she.

He admitted as much when, all the documents safely in his briefcase, he strolled with her back to her sitting room. She thought he might wait for a short moment before saying goodnight. And, though he did pause, it was not as a prelude to saying goodnight, but to all at once ask, 'How does your landlord feel about gentlemen callers staying the night?'

Her heart suddenly began to hammer. It was late, and she was tired, and it took every scrap of her remaining energy for her to keep her expression bland. Her pulse was leaping all over the place as she pondered—surely to heaven Joel wasn't thinking of sharing her bed!

'I haven't lived here long enough to find out. But—' She broke off to look pointedly at her sofa. 'If you think you'll be comfortable there, you're quite welcome.'

His lips twitched. As tired as he was, and she calculated he must have been on the go for close on twenty hours, his lips definitely twitched. But he took her up on her offer. 'I'd much prefer to rest my eyes here for an hour before I tackle the hours drive back to my place, if you wouldn't mind.'

Chesnie found him a blanket and a couple of pillows and, more than ready for bed herself, said 'Goodnight,' and, unused to having any male 'staying over', went hurriedly to her bedroom.

As exhausted as she was, though, sleep was elusive. She still felt restless, fidgety, and, she had to admit, emotional. Emotional without knowing why she should feel so. She couldn't hear one single, solitary sound coming from the sitting room, so presumed that Joel had gone 'spark out'.

Proof, however, that she too had gone 'spark out' at some time, came when she opened her eyes to find that it was six o'clock—and that Joel was in her room.

Joel was *in her room*! 'What...?' was as far as she could manage as, pushing a cloud of hair away from her face, she struggled to sit up.

'I did knock,' Joel informed her. 'You were sound asleep.'

'Er—yes. Well...' Her brain was still asleep—and he could hardly have had much more than three hours' sleep. That thought abruptly vanished when, startlingly, she suddenly became aware of her bare arms—the narrow straps of her nightdress no covering at all—and the front of her nightdress, more *décolleté* than *décolleté*—none of which was lost on Joel.

'I thought I'd mention I may be out of the office for most of today,' he stated, his glance flicking to where the tips of her breasts were showing dark through the fine white lace material. Hastily she pulled the covers up to her chin. He looked amused—she wanted to hit him! 'You'll have to rearrange my diary accordingly,' he instructed.

She'd had enough of him. 'Naturally I'll rearrange your diary!' she answered tartly, and, for good measure, 'Goodbye!'

He looked at her for perhaps one second longer, then commented nicely, 'If you're like this with all your gentlemen callers, it's no wonder none of them stay the night.'

With that he went, and she would dearly have loved to throw something after him. Good grief—what was wrong with her? She was feeling emotional again.

It was business as usual the next time she saw Joel. He made no mention of the comfort or otherwise of her sofa, for which she was very glad.

By Saturday her emotions were on a much more even keel, and she enjoyed dining with Philip. He did not refer again to his feelings for her and, given that he kissed her cheek on parting, his behaviour was impeccable.

On Sunday she drove to Cambridge to see her parents. She loved them both dearly, but had soon had too much of their bickering and was much relieved when the time came that she could say she had to get back.

That night she rang her grandfather. 'Dad tells me you've found the house you're looking for,' she said brightly, loving him to bits.

'It's only a two-up, with bathroom, and two-down, but it's sufficient for my needs.'

'You'll be wanting your car back?' she suggested.

'No hurry,' he replied. 'It'll be some time before the purchase is completed and I have the rest of my furniture out of storage. Now, how are you?'

Chesnie came away from the phone, her good spirits restored. She was earning better money now. She would start looking for a car at the first opportunity. Something small, and not too expensive.

Though when, she wondered, when the two weeks that followed saw her working late each night, would she ever find the time to go looking for a car? Although there were quite some months to go yet, things were already starting to warm up in the battle for who would win the chairmanship when Winslow Yeatman retired.

She had met all the other directors—Arlene Enderby was

a most frequent visitor to the office next door. Some were
directors by virtue of either being a Yeatman, marrying a
Yeatman, or, like Joel, working their way up by their own
merit.

Fergus Ingles was one such. He was not putting up for
chairman, and had not as yet declared which candidate he
was likely to support. Of late, Fergus had taken a leaf out
of Arlene Enderby's 'just popping in while passing' book.
But where Arlene popped in to see Joel, Fergus always
made a bee-line for Chesnie's desk.

On Friday he 'popped in' to see if she fancied going to
the theatre with him the next evening, and, having been
turned down, was just leaving when Joel came from his
office to discuss some matter with her.

The two men acknowledged each other, but Fergus had
barely closed the door after him when Joel was asking,
'What did Ingles want?' He didn't sound thrilled.

Chesnie stayed calm to reply, 'Someone to go to the
theatre with tomorrow.'

'Someone? Anyone?'

As ever, Joel wanted all the 'i's dotted and all the 't's
crossed, though Chesnie knew that he was quite well aware
that the invitation had been to her personally. 'Me,' she
admitted.

'You haven't time for a social life!' Joel told her sharply,
and just the preposterousness of that remark caused her to
break free of her cool image for once. She laughed out loud.
But clearly Joel didn't see anything to laugh at, and his
tone was sharp still when he barked, 'You're not going?'

Honestly! She slaved for this man—her free time was
her own. 'I might,' she replied. 'And then again, I might
not.' For her sins she was on the receiving end of a mur-
derous look, and Joel kept her working late that night.

In actual fact she loved her work, and didn't mind a bit
working overtime. 'Goodnight,' she said pleasantly, when
at last everything had been completed. He looked up and

seemed to study her intently, as if she was a new species to him. She smiled. 'Have a good weekend.'

But as she drove home she started to feel a little annoyed over the way Joel had seemed to take exception to the idea of her seeing one of the directors outside of work. Surely Joel didn't think Fergus would try and find out from her anything highly confidential Joel had told her with regard to his bid to be chairman? Surely Joel didn't think that she would be so indiscreet as to let anything slip? She began to feel exceedingly irritated—didn't Joel trust her?

Chesnie had dinner again with Philip Pomeroy the next night. But it was over that meal that she began to see that maybe Joel had some excuse to be a shade wary where PAs were concerned. She and Philip had been congenially chatting on and off through their meal when Philip suddenly looked at her, sighed very softly, and said, 'I know we have a pact not to talk business, Chesnie, but I've recently come across an item of news that just has to earn me a few stars if I share it with you.'

She looked back at him. 'Oh?' she queried warily.

'I'm not asking you to tell me anything,' he quickly assured her, 'but you might be interested to know I yesterday interviewed a woman named Deborah Sykes for the job as my PA.'

Deborah Sykes! Chesnie knew her. Until only a couple of weeks ago, when the company had found serious reasons to dispense with Deborah's services, she had been one of the senior PAs at Yeatman Trading.

'Oh, yes?' Chesnie answered non-committally, not certain she should be having this conversation with Philip. But since he had stated that he wasn't asking her to tell him anything she decided to stay with it—for the moment, anyhow. She felt she could trust Philip, but the minute this called for her to contribute something she would close the conversation down.

'As you're no doubt fully aware, Deborah Sykes was PA to Russell Yeatman until, by mutual agreement, they parted company.' From what Chesnie had heard there had been nothing mutual about it. 'What you are probably not aware of,' Philip went on when Chesnie made no reply, 'is that her boss—or should I say her ex-boss—while pretending to support your boss, Joel Davenport, is planning, when he feels the time is right, to put in his own bid to be chairman of Yeatman Trading.'

How Chesnie managed to keep her jaw from hitting the table in shock, she had no idea. She wanted to argue, wanted to tell Philip that he was mistaken, that Russell Yeatman was most definitely intending to support Joel when the time came to vote. But Philip wouldn't lie, and who had been closer to Russell Yeatman and in a position to see what went on other than Deborah Sykes—who'd been his PA?

'It was kind of Deborah to share that snippet with you,' Chesnie commented lightly.

'I rather gathered she thought it might help Symington Technology to know who was likely to be the next chairman of Yeatman Trading, and that I would be suitably grateful.'

'And offer her the job?' Chesnie suggested, her mind reeling at the implication that Russell Yeatman, because he was a Yeatman, might get the chairmanship. How dared he pretend to support Joel!

'A waste of time.'

'You didn't offer her the job?' Chesnie asked.

'Why would I want a PA who can't keep her mouth shut?'

Chesnie parted from Philip in her usual friendly manner that night, but she was glad to be alone—her head was still spinning with the implications of what Philip had told her. If he was right, and she was sure he was, then the most votes Joel was certain of were two. That meant there were six votes, including Russell Yeatman's vote, that could go against him. The present chairman's vote wouldn't need to be involved. If the Yeatmans wanted a Yeatman, it was a foregone conclusion that Russell Yeatman would win.

Chesnie spent Sunday with her mind in a turmoil. Should she phone Joel and tell him what she had learned? But he'd worked so hard that week. Surely he was entitled to one day of rest. Would he want to know anyway? Well, of course he would want to know. But perhaps he knew already. And what could he do about it anyhow?

In the end Chesnie decided against contacting Joel, but she went into the office early on Monday morning. As ever, Joel was in first. She went straight in to see him.

'Uh-oh, this looks ominous!' Joel said, looking up to observe her serious expression. 'If you've come in early to give me your resignation, I'm afraid I have to tell you I don't take resignations on Mondays.'

He smiled; she didn't. Something—or someone—had obviously put him in a good mood. She didn't want to consider what he might have been doing over the weekend.

There was only one way to say this. 'I've heard a whisper that you have serious competition for the chairmanship,' she stated flatly—and that took the good humour out of his face. She'd almost forgotten how very, very determined he was to have that chairmanship.

'The devil you have!' he retorted bluntly. 'Where did this whisper come from?' he demanded.

'Is it important where it came from?'

'Of course it's important!' he barked. And, apparently having not forgotten her visitor of Friday afternoon, 'Fergus Ingles!' he guessed. 'He told you? You went to the theatre with him on Saturday and he told you he intended to oppose me!'

'No, I didn't!' she denied crossly. 'And it isn't him. He isn't the one who's going against you—it's—Russell Yeatman.'

'Russell Y...' Joel stared at her in disbelief. 'You're seriously suggesting that Russell Yeatman has defected from my corner and intends to go for the chairmanship himself?'

'That's the way I heard it,' she confirmed.

'Where?' he demanded toughly. 'If you didn't hear it from Fergus Ingles, where did you hear it?'

Chesnie knew she was going to have to tell him. In order to gauge the strength of her source, Joel was going to have to know. 'I had dinner with Philip Pomeroy on Saturday—'

'Pomeroy! You're still consorting *occasionally* with the enemy?' Chesnie knew this Monday morning had started off badly, but was determined not to let Joel Davenport's sarcastic jibes get to her. That was until he went on, 'So what happened to the pact you had with him not to discuss my office business?'

'I did *not* discuss your business!' she flared.

'You had to tell him something to gain that little nugget!' he accused harshly—and Chesnie's usual grip on her temper went flying.

She had once before felt like walking out—she came close a second time. But, instead of walking, this time she stayed rooted. 'You don't fully trust me, do you?' she blazed. And, not giving him a chance to say yea or nay, she stormed angrily on. 'That much became clear last Friday, when you objected to the notion I might consider dating one of your fellow directors! Well, let me—' She broke off when she saw that Joel was looking at her with something that looked, if she wasn't mistaken, very much like admiration in his eyes. 'What...?' she challenged belligerently.

He rose to the challenge. 'Did you know that when you forget to look out at the world through your permafrost, your eyes sparkle like emeralds?'

She wanted to stay mad at him—but couldn't. 'Soft soap,' she muttered, supposing this was the reason he left a trail of PAs, and women in general, swooning in his wake. Though not her. Assuredly not her.

'I do trust you, Chesnie. If I didn't you wouldn't be working for me.' His expression was unsmiling. 'I apologise if anything I said on Friday upset you, and that goes double for this morning. I confess that what you've just told me has come as a bit of a bombshell.' He was still looking serious as he continued, 'If your news checks out I shall need to take some kind of drastic action. You'd better take a chair and tell me all you know.'

Chesnie became aware as that week progressed that Joel was keeping as much home-based as possible. She rather liked having him working in the next-door office, and had to admire the way in which he acted in the same outwardly affable way he'd always acted when Russell Yeatman, the man who was preparing to stab him in the back when his chance came, dropped by to see him.

What Chesnie did not enjoy was the way Arlene Enderby, who didn't even work there, director though she might be, seemed to appear in Joel's office on a daily basis. Arlene, without a doubt, as Joel's father had suggested, was still after him.

The fact, however, that Joel was not so keen on the idea of being chased became apparent to Chesnie on Friday, when Arlene rang to speak with him as he was about to leave the office for a meeting. Chesnie knew for a fact he had two minutes available in which to take the call. But, 'I'm not available,' he told Chesnie, and went.

'I'm afraid Joel's at a meeting. May I take a message?' Chesnie suggested tactfully, aware, as she was sure Joel must be, that if he wanted to court Arlene's chairmanship vote it wouldn't do to upset her.

'What time is he due back?' Arlene asked, a touch put out.

'He may go straight home from his meeting, but I can leave a message on his desk in case he comes back when I've gone,' Chesnie offered.

'Damn!' Arlene muttered. 'I wanted him to come to a party with me tomorrow. I suppose if I ring his home I shall only find myself talking to his answering machine.'

Arlene rang off, and Chesnie had several messages from other sources for Joel when he returned an hour later. She left telling him about Arlene Enderby's call till the end. '…and Arlene Enderby would like you to go to a party with her tomorrow,' Chesnie relayed nicely.

He took the message without so much as a blink, and asked, 'And what are your plans for tomorrow?'

'You want me to work?'

Joel looked at her with humour in his eyes. 'I don't deserve you,' he told her.

'True,' she answered—and loved it when they shared a small laugh together.

'I think you can have tomorrow off,' he said, after a moment, but hadn't lost sight of his original question, it seemed, when he rephrased it. 'Are you off partying tomorrow?'

'Tomorrow I'm off to visit my grandfather,' she stated.

'He lives where?'

'Herefordshire. He's in the process of buying a cottage,' she volunteered, then suddenly realised how well and truly she had departed from the cool image she was at pains to show the world. 'If you would just sign these letters, I'll get them in the post.' With that she turned and went back to her desk.

She knew she enjoyed seeing Joel laugh, enjoyed seeing him relax every now and then from his busy day. She by far preferred to see him that way than as the short, sharp, snarling brute he could be sometimes. And she knew she wanted to be on friendly terms with him—yet at the same time being on those amicable terms with him seemed somehow to make her feel strangely vulnerable—and she didn't want that.

Chesnie stayed overnight with her grandfather on Saturday, and together they inspected his new purchase. 'It's a delightful cottage, in a beautiful spot,' she replied when he asked her opinion.

'I think it's plenty big enough for me,' he said, and smiled as he added, 'I don't hold with too much housework. Although Mrs Weaver, a few doors down, has said she'll come in and give the place a "going over" whenever I give her a call.'

It was good to know that her grandfather would soon be settled in his own place. Chesnie drove back to London on Sunday, having assured herself that he was managing, and would be able to manage very well on his own. It was what he wanted. Since her grandmother's death he had become something of an insomniac. When he'd lived with her parents her mother had carped on about him getting up in the middle of the night to make himself a warm drink—he wasn't going to give up his independence again in a hurry.

Her visit to Herefordshire at the weekend was far from her mind on Tuesday. Arlene Enderby had outstayed her welcome in Joel's office yesterday, and Chesnie had picked up very clear vibes when she had gone in that Joel, wanting to get on with work which he considered of far greater importance, had been doing his best to shake her off. Arlene, clearly, was having none of it.

Arlene made a visit to his office again on Tuesday. A visit of which Chesnie was entirely unaware until, pausing only to stow her bag on her return from lunch, she walked over to the communicating door and went in. Arlene was there, and so too was Joel, but there was an odd sort of tension in the air. They were not looking at each other, but had turned and were looking at her.

All Chesnie's instincts were suddenly alert. Something was telling her to retreat. To leave the room, and to come back later. But, 'It's you!' Arlene suddenly exclaimed. 'It's you, isn't it?'

Chesnie hadn't a clue what she was talking about, and glanced swiftly to Joel—he glanced blandly back. But, like the professional she was, Chesnie thought she'd better show a cool front until she knew more of what Arlene Enderby was referring to. 'I—er…' What in creation was going on?

'Joel's just told me he's getting engaged, but won't say to who,' Arlene informed her, and while Chesnie felt distinctly shattered to know that Joel was to be engaged,

Arlene, plainly striving hard to hide how she felt at this news, had recovered sufficiently to state, 'He's said no to all the names I could think of—and then you came in.' Arlene turned back to him. 'It is Chesnie, isn't it?' she asked.

Chesnie's momentarily stunned brain at that point came out of its shock, and she was suddenly working at full brain power. Of course Joel wasn't getting engaged! He'd run like fury at the thought of getting that close to marriage. All too obviously Arlene had backed him into a corner, perhaps with yet another party invitation, and in order to kill any future invitations—or maybe to head off her chase, perhaps to let her down gently—he had fed her the line that he was going to get married. Arlene, not one to duck from asking questions, wanted to know who.

Chesnie allowed herself a small smile. She had seen Joel diplomatically handle quite a few difficult situations. She knew he was going to deny it, but she also knew it was going to take all his diplomacy skills to deny any attachment to her while at the same time keeping Arlene out of his hair.

Chesnie raised her eyes to look at him. She saw that his glance was on her mouth, but as she watched she saw that glance flick upwards, and suddenly he was looking straight into her green eyes. After a momentary pause, all at once he, too, was smiling. He'd thought up something good, Chesnie knew he had.

But she just could not believe her ears when, his glance moving to Arlene, he replied, 'We weren't going to say anything just yet...' He turned back to Chesnie and, still smiling, added, 'Were we, darling?'

That took the smile off her face. He surely hadn't said what she thought he had just said? She knew he hadn't. Chesnie didn't believe it! Couldn't believe it. But all at once Arlene Enderby was brilliantly hiding whatever her inner feelings were and had gone over to Joel to give him a kiss of congratulation.

'You'll have all the other PAs after your blood,' she turned to Chesnie to say lightly, and while Chesnie was having a hard time hiding her own feelings—only her years of practice aiding her to keep a calm front until she got to have a private word with her 'fiancé'—the door to her office opened. Unannounced, unexpected, Joel's father came in. It was all she needed.

'Magnus!' Arlene exclaimed, greeting him like some long-lost friend. Magnus started to walk through into his son's office. 'I suppose you knew all about Joel and Chesnie?' she trilled, going over and giving him a hug.

'What's this, then?' he asked when she let him go.

'Don't tell me you didn't know that Joel and Chesnie are engaged?'

Magnus's face lit up. 'I couldn't be more pleased!' he beamed, and came over to where Chesnie, wondering if the world had gone mad, was standing. For the moment she was somehow still managing to conceal her feelings, and stood rooted while Magnus gave her a kiss and exclaimed, 'I couldn't ask for a more terrific daughter-in-law!' And, while Chesnie was only just managing to mask her horror that she should be anybody's daughter-in-law, he went over and shook his son warmly by the hand.

'This calls for champagne!' Arlene declared.

Ye gods! Chesnie looked directly at Joel and guessed he must have read in her expression that she was about to burst a few blood vessels. 'This calls for Chesnie and me to get on with some work,' he stated unequivocally, but he still was smiling.

'Which means you and I will have to go off and drink champagne on our own, Arlene,' Magnus said, taking his son's hint wonderfully.

Chesnie thought they would never go. But eventually, after Joel's father gave her another kiss, they both departed. And with their departure so too did Chesnie's composure leave her.

'What on earth do you think you're playing at?' she

turned to Joel to demand the moment she heard the outer door close.

'It was your fault!' he tossed back at her, equally unsmiling.

The cheek! His sauce took her breath away. 'How?' she challenged. 'I've just come back from lunch! I didn't say a—'

'It was the way you *looked*!' Joel interrupted her. 'The smug way you smiled!' he told her bluntly. 'I'm just about up to here with one woman trying to manipulate me—then there are you too, believing you know exactly how I'll react.'

Chesnie had to admit that perhaps she had been a bit smug as she'd waited for him to 'diplomatically' own up to the truth of the matter. But she was still furious. 'I know you want Arlene's vote, but you—'

'For your information,' he chopped her off curtly, 'Arlene Enderby's a realist, and, regardless of whether it's a family member or not, she'll vote for whoever she believes will ultimately bring her the best rewards!'

'Whatever,' Chesnie snapped. 'That still doesn't give you the right, whether or not you're fed up with manipulative women and smug women, to say what you did.' And, unsure of Arlene's gossip level, but knowing his father's penchant for chatting freely on everything and everyone, 'It will be all over the building in two minutes!'

He shrugged. 'So, we'll deny it.'

'A fat lot of good that will do!' Chesnie erupted, outraged that he thought he could shrug it off and it would all blow over. 'We've been away together,' she charged on, digging her heels in when she could see she just wasn't getting through to him. And, while he did look a shade startled at what she had just said, she sought for something else to really make him sit up and take notice. 'You've stayed overnight in my flat!' she reminded him, when nothing else very clever presented itself.

That was sufficient, anyhow; she could tell that from the

astounded expression that came to his face. 'Hell's teeth!' he exclaimed, appalled, looking absolutely aghast. 'Surely you're not suggesting I should actually *marry* you!'

That hurt! The pain of it was stupefying. And the pain of what she had just realised rocked her. 'You should be so lucky!' she managed to slam back—before deciding she needed to hide. She turned from him and marched quickly out from his office, straight to the bottom drawer of her desk.

She didn't know Joel had come to the door and was watching her until, as she collected her bag and closed the drawer, he demanded 'Where are you going with that?'

Chesnie had a feeling she was going to break down any minute—and no man was going to do that to her. 'Home!' she retorted, afraid to say more lest her voice gave her away.

She had twice before come close to walking out. This time she went at speed—straight out from her office. She had resigned, and knew that she was never going back. How could she go back? She had only a few moments ago realised that she had fallen in love with Joel. In his book that was probably a sackable offence anyway!

CHAPTER FIVE

CHESNIE was in shock for the rest of the day. She went to bed that night still reeling. How had it happened—this love she had for Joel? This feeling that had exploded in on her so unannounced. Why hadn't she seen it coming? Had she done so, then surely she could have taken some evasive action.

Oh, she liked him. Most of the time she liked him quite a lot. She admired him tremendously too; the man positively ate work. But—love him? She shook her head—oh, that it would so easily go away. But it wouldn't, and she knew that it wouldn't. It was there, this love she had for Joel and she could do absolutely nothing about it.

Over and over that night, as she lay in her bed, Chesnie relived that scene that had led up to her walking out of her job. That job she loved so much. She tried to get angry with Joel. How dared he, with that, 'We weren't going to say anything just yet. Were we, darling?' confirm for Arlene Enderby that he and his PA were *engaged*.

And what about Arlene Enderby? Joel plainly knew her to be hard-headed enough to vote where it might affect her bank balance. Equally plain was that for him to have used the desperate excuse he had to shake her off must mean he had used up all other reasons to stop her from chasing him. Chesnie supposed that she had appeared at just the wrong moment, and her smug look must have been the last straw as far as Joel was concerned.

But—engaged! No, it was too much. Even though Chesnie was sure that by now Joel would have put the word out that there was absolutely not the slightest truth in any despicable rumour that he and his PA were engaged,

Chesnie thought it too much. Once that rumour had got round it was not going to be so easy to scotch. And 'engaged' spelled commitment. And commitment in that area spelled disaster. Love him she might, but Chesnie wanted no part of it.

She got up the next morning at her usual time, but with her anger spent. It was negated by the fact that she would never work with Joel again. Negated by the fact that he would not want her to work in his office. By walking out she had walked out on all chance of ever seeing him. And that hurt.

That Wednesday was a most unhappy day for Chesnie. It seemed to drag by endlessly slowly. The logic of her head told her that what she should be doing was getting out there and finding herself another job. So far as she knew that job in Philip's office was still open. But she didn't want to work for Philip, and nor did she wish to listen to logic. She could easily have telephoned one of her sisters and arranged lunch somewhere, or have spent the day searching for a car, but she didn't have the heart to do any of those things. What she wanted to do was what she did—stay home to lick her wounds in private.

She did see someone before that day was out, though. It was just after eight that evening when the outer buzzer sounded. She ignored it; she didn't want to see anyone.

The buzzer sounded a second time. Surely if it was Nerissa she would have telephoned first? Though perhaps not if she was in something of a 'fume' over her husband's latest misdemeanour. Not wanting her sister to have had a wasted journey, Chesnie went out into the hall. 'Hello?' she said into the intercom.

'Are you still sulking?' questioned an all-male voice.

Joel! Wonderful Joel! Before she had thought about it, joy in her heart after such a miserable day, Chesnie had pressed the button to let him into the building. Then, when she did get round to thinking about it, a dozen other thoughts flashed through her mind. Joel—here! Her hair!

She who had previously had little to do with vanity, raced to her bedroom. Did she look all right? She ran a comb through her lovely red-blonde hair and tucked her silk shirt more neatly into the waistband of her tailored trousers. Her doorbell sounded before she could do any more. Joel was here! Why had he come? She wasn't ready to see him again. Yes, she was. A day without seeing him had been unbearable.

She hurried to the door. Calm, she instructed before she opened it. Be calm, be cool, be composed. Those were the instructions she gave herself. Then she opened the door, and there he was, the man she loved, tall, straight, good-looking, and her insides went like jelly.

She couldn't speak, she turned away, and Joel followed her into her sitting room. When she felt she had a tighter grip on her emotions she turned, but, still not trusting herself to speak, she instead gave him what she hoped was a cool, questioning look.

He looked back equally unspeaking, his glance going over her trim but curvy shape, taking in her shining hair and coming to rest on the face he had called lovely.

Seconds passed. She saw his glance flick to her mouth, and she wanted to swallow—but that would be letting the side down. 'To what do I owe this unexpected pleasure?' she asked, when she could bear his inspection, the silence, no longer.

He smiled, and she found a little bit of hate for him. He, by his very silence, had made her speak. 'I thought I'd better call in person,' he said pleasantly. 'We've had an invitation to dine with Winslow and Flora Yeatman.'

The chairman and his wife! *We!* 'Didn't you tell them I no longer work for you?' she responded.

He smiled again, a charming smile. It was a smile she did not trust. And was right not to trust, she discovered, when, coolly, he replied, 'We weren't invited in that capacity.'

What other capacity was th—? Her eyes widened in

shock, that *we* starting to make sense. 'You...' she said on a gasp of sound. She couldn't believe it. But, it had to be, didn't it? She did swallow then—there was only one way to find out. 'Are you saying,' she began slowly, 'that you have not yet corrected the impression that you and I—are engaged?'

'What sort of a cad do you take me for?' he enquired silkily, and at that hint of devilment in his eyes she knew that he was playing with her. Why, she couldn't fathom—unless, of course, he hadn't taken too kindly to her walking out on him and leaving him without the assistant he needed.

'What do you mean?' she flared.

'What would I mean?' he answered smoothly, his blue gaze taking in the angry sparks in her wide green eyes. 'Surely it's the woman's place to announce to everybody that she's ditched her man.'

'D-ditched...'

'It would be the height of caddishness, surely, should I be the one to tell everyone that I was the one who did the ditching.'

Chesnie, recovering slightly, did not thank him for his consideration, and rounded on him angrily. 'In the first place, you are not "my man". In the second place, but for me covering for you when your love-life blew up in your face—'

'Hardly my love-life,' he butted in. 'Nor did you cover for me—you just stayed smugly and silently watching, while you waited to see how I was going to handle a tricky situation.' He shrugged nicely. 'So I handled it—we got engaged.'

'We were never engaged!' she erupted. 'Nor are we engaged.'

'That's not the talk at the forum,' he replied charmingly.

'You're saying...?' She couldn't finish it.

Joel had no such problem. 'As you rightly suggested, word about "us" spread like wildfire.' Oh, no! His words winded her, and she had to struggle to find a modicum of

her former outward composure. But then, having all but
floored her, 'Well?' he enquired evenly. 'Will you come
with me?'

'Where to?' she asked, still feeling stunned.

'Dinner with Winslow and Flora,' he reminded her—and
at his so easily asked enquiry some of her former spirit
returned.

'No, I won't!' she erupted.

'Why not?' he asked, sounding so reasonable—making
it seem as though she was the unreasonable one—that she
wanted to hit him.

'What—and further perpetuate this myth that you and I
are engaged? Why would you want to anyway?'

'I don't want to,' Joel answered, confirming what she
already knew. 'It's just that the Yeatmans have such a
happy marriage. Flora has kind of picked up the ball and
run with it—she's in raptures that I appear to have at last
been snared.'

'Snared!' Chesnie exclaimed, affronted. There was more
here than he was saying. It was probably all to do with
business, but she was too churned up just then to be able
to work it out. That word 'snared', however, just as if she'd
trapped him, caused her pride to furiously rear up. Who did
he think he was? What about *her* being snared? She set
about showing him that she had offers of her own and
didn't need to 'snare' any man. 'Apart from the fact that
you and I are not engaged—or ever likely to be—what
about my present relationship?'

'You mean—there's some other man?' Joel questioned,
and Chesnie knew that if he carried on like this for very
much longer she was definitely going to have to hit him!
She saw his glance go round her sitting room, as if searching for some evidence that she had a man about the place.
Of course there wasn't so much as the merest sign. His
glance came back to her. 'Trust me, you won't have time
to conduct a relationship.'

'I—won't?' she questioned, not with him at all.

Joel shook his head. 'Not while you're working for me. Things are hotting up.'

Things were hotting up? He had to be meaning the fight for the chairmanship. Chesnie suddenly glared at him—she had actually been thinking in terms of helping all she could! 'I'm not working for you!' she exploded.

'Ah, Chesnie,' he murmured softly, 'don't say that. You know you've been bored out of your skull staying home all day today.'

That was true—the day had stretched interminably. It occurred to her to wonder, *if* she went back to work for him, if she would be so busy she wouldn't have time to think about her feelings for him. 'So I'll stay bored!' She refused to give in to the weakness of love that, foolish though it was, still made her want to see him every day.

Joel heaved a dramatic sigh, and came a couple of paces closer. 'You want me to tell you that I can't cope without you?' he asked, close enough to look steadily into her eyes. 'You want me to tell you that already the office is falling apart? Without you there at—'

Oh, she did love him so. 'I'd love it,' she butted in, and—against all inclination—she just had to laugh.

Joel's eyes went to her mouth and, as if he enjoyed seeing her laugh, his own mouth started to curve upwards. 'Come back, Chezz,' he urged softly, and, unhurriedly coming those few steps closer, took a light hold of her upper arms. As if to add weight to his request, he placed a light kiss on her cheek.

Her control was instantly shot. Just the feel of his wonderful mouth against her cheek and, shaken rigid by his spontaneous kiss, his unexpected hold, Chesnie was desperately fighting to regain her shattered control.

Swiftly she pushed him away, and more than ever needed the cool front which over the years had become second nature to her. She found help in her struggle that, when she pushed him away, Joel immediately let go his hold on her arms.

She was still recovering her composure when, 'What do you say?' Joel pressed. 'A life at some boring other job, or a return to the demanding job you love? Say yes,' he urged.

'I...' she faltered. Yes, the work was demanding, and did sometimes stretch her, but... Chesnie made the mistake of looking at him—and was weakened. Oh, how could she deny herself the chance of seeing him every day? 'I'll—er—I'll come back, on one condition,' she agreed, her nerve-ends still all of a jangle.

'Name it,' he replied promptly.

'You ever kiss me again, Joel Davenport, and I'll walk out on you permanently.'

Solemnly he studied her. Then silently his hand came out to shake on it. 'I'll see you in the morning,' he agreed, shook hands with her—and went striding from her apartment.

Chesnie collapsed into a chair the moment he had gone, a hand going up to touch the side of her face that he had kissed. She loved him, and had given in to the weakness of love, and—she couldn't regret it. She loved him, and would see him again tomorrow.

The next day dawned bright and beautiful and Chesnie drove to Yeatman Trading full of enthusiasm for her work. The day did not go well. For one thing Joel had left her apartment the previous evening with the only issue resolved being that she was going to continue working for him.

The issue of their 'engagement', however, had not been resolved. What Joel told Winslow Yeatman when he said they would not be accepting his invitation to dinner was, she had decided, entirely up to Joel. For her part, and at the very first opportunity, she intended to stop any rumours that she and Joel were engaged.

Unfortunately, her first chance came when, Joel out of the office and not expected back for a couple of hours, one of the directors came in. Muriel Yeatman, a square-set, mid-fifties woman whom Chesnie had met before, had come purposely, it seemed, to wish her well on her engagement. The unfortunate part was that Arlene Enderby came in with her aunt, thereby putting Chesnie in a dilemma about what she wanted to do, and what, for Joel, she had to do.

'Isn't it wonderful, Aunty?' Arlene gushed when Muriel had said how delighted they all were by the news. And while Chesnie had to give Arlene top marks for covering whatever she was feeling about Joel now being out of her orbit, Chesnie was left with little choice but to go along with it—if she didn't want to let Joel down.

For a short while after they had gone Chesnie mutinied against Joel. Why in thunder couldn't he have told the predatory Arlene straight out that he wasn't interested in her and would she please stop coming to his office, wasting his time?

Very probably, in the politest way he knew, he already had, came back the answer. But precisely because Arlene *was* predatory, and once she had set her sights on him wouldn't so easily give up, it hadn't worked. So he'd invented a steady girlfriend—and don't forget *smug*.

Vowing never to be 'smug' ever again, Chesnie got on with her work—whenever she could. She was interrupted many times that day, Muriel Yeatman being not the only director of Yeatman Trading to call by and offer their good wishes on her engagement.

Heartily wishing that she had sorted out something, *anything*, with Joel before this—simply because half of the directors happened to be Yeatmans, and thereby related to Arlene Enderby—Chesnie saw that there was nothing for it but to go along with it until she had chance to talk to Joel.

He was back in the office just after two, but with little time to spare before he went off to his next appointment. Chesnie did not care—this matter had to be settled—*now*.

She went into his office with some data he would need to take with him, and after a few minutes of business discussion she informed him bluntly, 'Muriel Yeatman came in to wish me well on our engagement.'

Joel paused in placing the papers in his briefcase, and turned to study her stubborn expression. 'And you said?'

'What could I say? Arlene Enderby came in with her!'

'Ah!' He smiled then. 'I know I don't deserve such loyalty, but thank you, Chesnie.'

'That's not good enough!' she erupted, refusing to be charmed. 'They weren't the only directors to call in with their good wishes. What in creation am I supposed to say?'

'Why say anything?' he replied, his expression as serious as hers. 'By the sound of it, very few people haven't heard about "us".' He thought for a moment and then, clearly having no time to set about denying it, 'It will only be a nine-day wonder,' he decided, 'then something else will happen to take precedence.'

'You think our "engagement" will so easily be forgotten?' she asked, incredulous at his attitude.

'Of course,' he stated confidently, and, his mind plainly more on the importance of his work than on the unimportance of a mere matter of an engagement, 'Take my word for it, the whole business will die a natural death—especially when you and I show no sign of taking that diabolical trot up the aisle.' He paused to take a quick glance to his watch. 'Back around four,' he said, and was gone.

Chesnie was still staring after him, dumbstruck that he could be so unconcerned, when business called for her attention in the shape of a ringing telephone.

She had little time herself during that afternoon in which to give the matter much thought. As Joel had said, things were hotting up, and she was working flat out to cope. She had a brief moment to suppose that, as Joel had so quaintly put it, when they didn't show any signs of trotting up the aisle all talk of them being engaged would probably fizzle out—she only hoped it would 'fizzle' this week rather than next. Then it was all work.

As well as dealing with the general day-to-day business

of seeing to it that Joel's office ran on supremely smooth-oiled wheels, Chesnie had the previous day and half's work to catch up on. The interruptions she'd had that morning did not help.

She was still catching up on Friday afternoon, and it was a matter of pride to her that she had all her work completed so she should start with a clear desk come Monday.

At four-thirty she knew she was just not going to be able to make her date with Philip that night. That did not particularly bother her, other than she did not like to let people down. They had been going to a party some friends of Philip were giving, but she had been wondering more and more of late if it wouldn't be kinder to him in the long run if she told him it would be better if she didn't see him again.

She looked through to the other office. The door had been open for the last hour, while Joel needed to frequently check over some details. With that job out of the way she would have liked to get up and close the door, knowing that because of Philip being a competitor Joel didn't care for her going out with him. But she suddenly found she was feeling a touch rebellious. Tough! A slave for Davenport she might be, but he didn't own her. She picked up the phone, asked for an outside line, and dialled.

'Mr Pomeroy, please—Chesnie Cosgrove,' she informed the telephonist and, her eyes on the man making notes in the other room, she saw his pen momentarily pause before moving on. Then Philip was on the line and she tried to forget that Joel was very likely tuned in. 'I'm sorry to call this late,' she apologised to Philip, 'but I'm afraid I'm just not going to be able to make the party with you tonight. I had a day off on Wednesday,' she excused, 'and I'm still catching up.'

'You weren't ill?' Philip questioned in concern.

'No, no. I've been fine.' She smiled.

'Good. We can go to the party late,' he suggested. 'They won't mind.'

'I'd rather not.'

'How about tomorrow?'

'I'm sorry. I'm going to my parents for the weekend,' she explained, and for no reason glanced at the man in the other office. And he'd said *she* had looked smug! Joel Davenport was obviously delighted that his work had put a stop to her going out with Philip.

When she reached her flat that night Chesnie felt too exhausted to do anything but flop into bed. Almost a whole week had gone by and she had done nothing about buying herself a car—perhaps she'd find a minute next week in which to go car-hunting.

After a good night's sleep she felt recovered, and drove to her old home with Joel taking over her thoughts.

The weekend went pretty much as expected. Her parents were as tetchy with each other as ever, and Chesnie wasn't sorry to see Sunday morning arrive. On her way home she called in on her sister Robina—now back with her husband—and still had Robina's complaints about her philandering husband ringing in her ears when, because her sister Tonia would never forgive her if she didn't call on her too, she stopped in to have a cup of tea. Nerissa phoned her shortly after Chesnie reached her apartment, to chat and enquire about her latest 'doings'. But to neither her parents nor any of her sisters did she mention her 'nine-day wonder' of an engagement, or the fact that—quite ridiculously, she owned—she had fallen hopelessly in love with her non-fiancé.

Philip also telephoned her that evening, and her thoughts on not seeing him again caused her to want to tell him as much. 'Shall I see you on Saturday?' he asked, and the words to explain her decision hovered on her lips.

The only man she wanted to see on Saturday was Joel, and... Suddenly her pride gave her a sharp nudge. What the blazes did she think Joel would be doing on Saturday? Sitting at home thinking of her? Get real!

'I'd like that,' she told Philip before she could think further.

Chesnie spent some time on Monday morning reorganising Joel's already fully scheduled diary when he needed to find an extra hour to see someone in connection with one of their subsidiaries. He also needed to fit in an unexpected invitation to lunch with Edward King the following day. Edward King was a fellow senior director who had married a Yeatman. Chesnie knew Joel valued Edward's opinion, but as yet was uncertain if he had Edward's vote. Joel was already working under pressure—admittedly he seemed to enjoy it—and Chesnie saw it as her role to ease that tension whenever and wherever she could.

He had just gone off to his lunch with Edward King the next day when she received a phone call that caused her to realise Joel now had pressure of a different kind. Though she was sure it was nothing which he couldn't handle. His father rang.

'How's my daughter-in-law to be?' he asked cheerfully—and Chesnie knew panic. Instinctively she wanted to tell him that there was not the remotest possibility that she would be his daughter-in-law, and that she and his son were not engaged, and never had been.

'Magnus—' she even began, then, homing in to cause her to check was her knowledge of what a gossipy chatterbox he was—and he was on friendly terms with Arlene Enderby. Chesnie changed her mind to ask, 'How are you?'

'Extremely happy!' he replied. 'But I'd be even happier if you agreed to take your poor old near dad-in-law to lunch.'

She winced. She liked him. He was a bit of a rogue, a bit of a love, but while everything in her urged her to tell him the truth, and to tell him now, loyalty to Joel kept her silent. She would have to clear it with Joel first.

'I can't make lunch today,' she told Magnus, feeling relief that, because Joel was probably going to take an extended lunch hour, she needed to be back in the office 'holding the fort' by two.

'Oh.' He sounded disappointed. 'I was looking forward to seeing you.' He attempted to persuade. 'I'm happy, but still a bit lonely.'

He piled it on. And she fell for it. 'How would tomorrow suit? I could have lunch with you tomorrow,' she offered.

'I'll call for you,' he promptly accepted.

Which, as they said goodbye, caused Chesnie to know that Magnus would have to be told the truth before tomorrow. He was part of Joel's family, for goodness' sake. Joel's father. And Joel would obviously see that it was only right his father should be told.

So why was she feeling so churned up inside? she wondered when at three-fifteen she heard Joel enter his office. Come on, don't be absurd, do it. Do it now.

Chesnie took a deep breath, got to her feet, dithered for a split second and then, repeating, 'Absurd', she walked quickly across the carpet. With her chin up, her cool persona firmly to the fore, she opened the door and went in.

Oh, how she loved him—a chink appeared in her cool persona. 'Good lunch?' she enquired pleasantly.

He looked back at her. 'Thought-provoking,' he answered, his eyes on her still, a touch speculatively, she rather thought. Instead of enquiring, Any messages? which was what he sometimes did, and which would give her a lead to say that his father had telephoned, Joel invited, 'Take a seat.'

Drat. He sat one side of the desk; she took a seat across from him. She was interested in the 'thought-provoking' lunch he'd had with Edward King, but at the same time there were priorities here and, having built herself up to say what she had to say, suddenly it wouldn't wait.

'Your father rang,' she stated crisply.

'He upset you?' Joel asked, perhaps taking from her manner, for all she was trying to cover it, that she was in a tiny bit of a stew about something.

'Not at all!' she replied quickly. 'That is, he invited me to lunch, and though I couldn't go today, because I didn't want to leave the office, I—' She broke off. *Get it said, do.* 'I'm having lunch with him tomorrow and I think he should be told, before then, that you and I—that w-we are not engaged.' There. It was out. But Joel was already shaking his head—and that annoyed her. It was *his* problem, for heaven's sake, not hers! 'In fact,' she continued, spurred on because she didn't seem to be getting through to him, 'I think it would be very much better all round if you told everyone, right now, that we were never engaged in the first place.'

Joel looked at her for long moments, then, 'Oh, Chesnie,' he said. And while her 'cool' was shot, his was there by the bucketload. 'I'm afraid I can't do that.'

Taken aback, she stared at him. She knew that his work came first, but surely just a whisper in the right ear would start a counter-rumour going. 'You—can't?' she questioned, somehow starting to feel that there was more going on here than Joel just trying to politely get rid of the predatory Arlene. 'Why can't you?' Chesnie demanded, but, looking at him, saw in his expression something that hinted she might not like what she was about to hear.

'I cannot,' he began, his eyes nowhere but on her, 'because, point one, you won't be lunching with my father tomorrow.'

'I—won't?' she queried, mystified.

Joel shook his head. 'I have to go to Glasgow tomorrow. I want you with me. Point two,' he went on as she took on board that she would again be rearranging his diary, 'far from wanting to be released from my engagement...' *His* engagement! '...I'm being pressured to get married.'

Staggered, Chesnie stared at him. 'Why?' She asked the one question her intelligence had managed to bring her.

Joel shrugged, but staggered her further when he openly explained, 'Over lunch Edward confirmed what you and I already know, that Russell Yeatman intends to put himself up for the chairmanship. What we—I—didn't know until lunchtime, when Edward revealed his hand, is that Edward is going to vote for me, and that Winslow, our present chairman, has confided his belief that I'm the best man for the job.'

Chesnie's eyes never left Joel's face. She was truly delighted that Edward King had revealed his colours and was going to vote for Joel. And, casting her mind over the other candidates, she knew—her love for Joel aside—that, as Winslow Yeatman had said, Joel really was the best man for the job.

'But?' she questioned, knowing that there had to be more to it than that—what on earth did this have to do with Joel being pressured to get married?

'But, as you rightly ask, should it come to a split vote—and bearing in mind that out of eight available directors' votes, excluding my own, I have a guarantee of only three votes so far—with Winslow having the casting vote, he has confided in Edward that because of his love of family Winslow will only vote for a man who is married.'

Chesnie was staggered anew, and was fighting to see this matter objectively. Russell Yeatman, while being childless, was, she knew, married. She almost asked Joel if he wanted the chairman's job so badly he'd be prepared to marry to get it. But she knew that he did. Joel was ambitious, she had known that. He wanted the chairman's job and now looked to have an excellent chance of getting it. Particularly since—subject to him being married—he would have the present chairman's backing.

Chesnie felt quite ill at the thought of Joel being married, but she did not want his astute brain picking up so much as a glimmer of how she felt about him. Which left her with little option but to suggest, 'It sounds to me as though you'd better start looking in your little black book.'

'I don't need to,' he answered, his blue-eyed gaze holding her eyes.

'Y-you've found someone to marry?' she queried, hardly

knowing how she managed to keep her voice level. She was hurting and, love her job as she did, didn't know how she would be able to take working for him when he married.

His eyes were still holding hers when, staggeringly, he calmly replied, 'I'm looking at her.'

Which left Chesnie staring at him dumbstruck. 'You're…!' she gasped. Then, like a lightning bolt, what he was saying suddenly hit her—and she woke up with a bang. 'Oh, no!' she bluntly, angrily replied, and was on her feet.

'Why not?' he asked calmly, getting to his feet too and watching her across his desk.

'Why not?' She could hardly believe her hearing. How could he say what he had just said and remain so calm, so cool? 'I'm your PA and nothing else!' she exploded, slowly getting over the shock. 'What you've just suggested comes under the heading ''Beyond the call of duty''!'

'Think about it,' he suggested. 'We—'

'There's nothing to think about!' she interrupted hotly.

'What are you getting so stewed up about?' he wanted to know.

'You don't consider what you've just said anything to get *stewed up* about? You know perfectly well that I'm not remotely interested in being married.'

'Which is all to the good, surely?'

Chesnie was about to flare up again, but his question halted her. 'How?' she asked.

'You don't want marriage because you've seen too many marriages end in disaster. But we would know in advance how our marriage would end—no hurt on either side.'

She felt too churned up inside to cope with whatever logic that was supposed to be, so asked hostilely instead, 'Why should I marry you?'

'Because you know I'm the right man for the chairman's job. From comments you've made I've seen that you recognise I'm the more likely candidate to move this company forward than any of the others.' She couldn't argue against any of what he said. 'I think you'd enjoy being the chairman's PA too,' he added with a small smile.

Emotion started to get to her. The fact that she too would take that top rung of the promotion ladder passed her by. Joel *was* the right man, the best man for the job, for the company and its employees; she knew that. But marriage? No! Definitely no!

She gathered he had seen from her expression that she wasn't to be swayed when he took another tack and questioned, 'Apart from not wanting a husband, do you have some other reason? Your affair with Pomeroy?' he prompted.

'I'm not having an affair with him!' she denied hotly.

Whether Joel believed her or not she couldn't tell, but, whatever, he used her reply to his advantage. 'There you are, then—there's nothing to stop you.'

Confound him! Where did he get his nerve? 'Why should I?'

'Why shouldn't you?' he answered, managing to make what he proposed sound quite reasonable as he added, 'You practically live with me now.'

'I'm not going to live with you!' she erupted yet again, and saw him smile—every bit as if, while not agreeing to live with him, she was seriously considering marrying him. 'I'm not!' she repeated firmly—and saw that she just wasn't getting through to him.

She was especially not getting through to him when just then his phone rang. 'Sleep on it,' he suggested. 'We're in Glasgow tomorrow—we'll discuss it over dinner tomorrow evening.'

She opened her mouth to tell him that there was nothing to discuss. But when he did her the courtesy of continuing to ignore the phone her more controlled PA self got the better of her, and, without another word, she marched back to her own office—giving him space to take the call.

Back at her desk her head was a riot with all that had

been said; she wasn't having lunch with Magnus tomorrow, she was flying unexpectedly up to Scotland, and she was having dinner with Joel tomorrow, where they would discuss getting married!

She seemed to be working on autopilot as she made the flight arrangements, made their hotel reservation and took sundry phone calls. Later that afternoon she telephoned Joel's father to tell him that she couldn't lunch with him tomorrow after all.

'I know,' he answered, sounding quite cheerful about it. 'Joel gave me a ring and said he was heading north tomorrow. Naturally he wanted you with him.' Grief!

Chesnie felt she was sinking deeper into the quagmire. She was glad to be busy, but felt she just couldn't cope with all Joel had given her to 'sleep on' and run his office efficiently as well. She gave up thinking about the fusillade of shock he had showered her with, and concentrated on that which she was paid to do.

Why, when at six-fifteen she had cleared her desk and was ready to go home, she should feel awkward about going in to see him, she didn't know. If anyone should feel awkward it should be him.

Adopting a cool, calm outer being, she went quickly into the next-door office. Joel looked up from what he was doing. 'Off home?' he enquired affably.

'Unless there's anything…?'

He shook his head. 'Are you all right for transport to the airport in the morning? I could pick you up and—'

'No need to get carried away!' she interrupted crisply, recalling quite clearly how, on their last Scottish trip, he had merely asked her if she knew the way to the airport. 'I've got my grandfather's car—and the answer's still no.'

He smiled, and she had one of her 'hating' moments. 'We'll talk about it tomorrow,' he decreed. Without another word she turned about and left him.

Chesnie had been home barely half an hour when she admitted to be feeling oddly dissatisfied with her lot. It was all Joel's fault—it had to be; he'd unsettled her. She glanced around her sitting room. She had been happy here. And would continue to be happy here, she decided firmly. Yet somehow she felt in need of a change. Something, perhaps, to take her out of this rut.

This rut! She hadn't felt in a rut until today! Unsettled, yes. Falling in love with Joel had truly unsettled her. She'd tried not to think of him, but so much for trying. He was in her head the whole of the time.

How dared he create such havoc in her well-ordered life by suggesting they marry? Oh, she could quite well see why he was prepared to marry. Without question ambitious, and given he worked like a Trojan, Joel would let little stand in the way of his getting to the top. If he had to take a wife to achieve his ambition to get there, so be it.

But why would she want to marry him? In general—well, that was before today, she qualified—she had been quite happy with her lot. True, she loved him, and wanted to help him get what he had worked so hard towards. And it was also true that she didn't know anyone better to do the chairman's job—but to *marry* him!

She went to bed. Sleep on it, he had suggested. Who could sleep with that buzzing around in her head?

Though quite when she started to fear that if she did not marry him then Russell Yeatman, or even his cousin, Aubrey Yeatman, might get the chairmanship, neither having the drive and energy Joel had, she was unsure.

She thought about the family closing ranks against Joel, and did not like it. He deserved this job; she knew he did. Yes, but—to marry him? For heaven's sake, don't even consider it. The man was Romeo personified—well, he'd have to stop that for a start! At that point Chesnie just had to laugh. Grief, she wasn't going to marry him and that was that—even if it were true that there had been fewer females phoning him just lately.

A couple of hours later and Chesnie was still wide awake, having gone around and around in circles, and was still striving hard to convince herself not to get involved. If only she didn't love the wretched man, there wouldn't *be* any problem.

But she did love him, and she did want to help him. But she didn't want a husband. Her sisters had been along that route, and look what a disaster area their marriages were.

Yes, but, as Joel had said, she would know in advance how their marriage would end. So, plainly he was only thinking in terms of a brief marriage, while he got himself firmly secure in the role of chairman, and then—no hurt on either side, so he'd said—presumably they would divorce.

Given that her emotions were involved, Chesnie tried her hardest to look at the matter logically. It was a fact that she had no intention of ever marrying. So, given that she had nothing planned to do with her life for the next year—other than to prove herself the best PA going—would it hurt her to go through a ceremony of marriage with him?

What, precisely, would be different in her life, say in a year or so's time, from what was happening in her life now? Presumably she would still be working for Joel. The only difference being that they had been married, but were now divorced.

On that thought her eyelids started to droop. She didn't fool herself that Joel would ever fall in love with her. She sighed as sleep came to claim her. Joel wasn't interested in any long-term relationship. But then, neither was she.

CHAPTER SIX

CHESNIE was relieved on Wednesday to be too busy to think of personal matters. She flew to Glasgow with Joel and spent the morning in his office there, then attended a very involved and protracted meeting with him in the afternoon, where she took the minutes.

They eventually returned to their hotel some time after seven. She felt pretty drained, so had a fair idea how Joel, who'd led the discussions, must be feeling.

'I've a few matters to go through with you before I leave you in the morning,' he said, as they stepped out of the lift and walked along the corridor to where she had her room and he had his suite. 'Would you mind if we had dinner sent up?'

Her heart warmed to him. Clearly he needed space to unwind, and since he wasn't home, where better than his suite? 'I could do with relaxing a little myself,' she answered lightly.

And felt adrenalin start to pump when he looked down into her eyes and commented, 'We're so in tune.'

Chesnie parted from him and went to freshen up, beginning to feel a little churned up inside. As single-minded as ever, Joel had not said a word all day about his proposal. In fact, so single-minded had he been about the work they were there to do, she felt she could be forgiven for believing no such proposal had ever been voiced.

But, he *had* suggested what he had, just as he had said they would discuss it over dinner tonight—and she was starting to feel anxious. Yesterday she had dismissed the idea out of hand. Today, having 'slept on it', having thought and thought *and* thought, she had gone from a

'Couldn't possibly. It was unthinkable' to be tripped up by her love for him. She still had no wish to marry—but Joel was far more worthy of that job than anyone. And he wanted it badly. Did she love him enough to marry him to help him get it?

She reckoned she had done a fair bit of 'in depth' thinking, not to mention enough thinking 'round in circles' to last her the next decade. She did not want to think any more, and as soon as she was ready, having changed into black trousers and a crisp white shirt, she left her room.

Joel had taken a quick shower too, she observed from his damp hair. 'What do you fancy to eat?' he asked courteously, inviting her into the sitting room of his suite. He had soon phoned down their order, and while they were waiting for it he went over some complicated work detail which, as well as typing back the minutes, she would be doing the next morning while he went off on other work pursuits.

Their meal arrived and, with work out of the way, Joel kept the conversational ball rolling—on any subject except the one which Chesnie was beginning to think he had changed his mind about.

She started to really relax then, and began to talk freely, conversationally, herself, delighting in his company. She savoured those moments, and sipped the last of her coffee knowing that very shortly, nothing said, she would return to her room.

And then it was that Joel, glancing from her lips, which were showing a natural smile rather than the more guarded smile she allowed, commented, 'We've had a hectic and tiring day, Chesnie. But before I let you go...' his glance was now steady on her green eyes '...have you an answer for me?'

On that instant her throat went dry. 'An an-answer?' she stammered chokily.

'I suggested we marry,' he reminded her, when she needed no reminding at all.

'Oh,' she mumbled, and, looking at him, loved him so much. 'Er—for how long would it be?'

'Two years at the most,' Joel replied promptly. 'I'd need time once I've won the chairmanship to show what I can do. Once I've done that, my position should be secure.'

Two years was a long time! 'I wouldn't want to be married for any longer,' she said.

'Does that mean you've just said yes?'

Oh, help. 'You could be celibate for two years?' she asked, instinctively feeling then that in the circumstances she should marry him, but unable to help feeling a touch panicky all the same.

'Celibate?' Joel enquired in surprise, to her ears sounding as though he had never heard the word before.

Chesnie felt herself going a little pink. She strove hard for something of her cooler image, and needed it as she explained, 'Well, obviously you and I...I mean, our marriage—if we do get married,' she inserted hurriedly, 'will end at the—um—bedroom door.' Joel looked interested, but didn't comment or interrupt, allowing her to struggle on to the very end. 'While, of course, ours will be a marriage of convenience only, I couldn't put up with a m-man who...' her voice was fading, but she made herself go on, '...who took his pl-pleasures elsewhere.'

'Two years?' Joel queried. This was clearly something he had not given a moment's thought. But, 'Very well,' he agreed, after some careful consideration. And in turn surprised her by asking, 'And you?'

'Me?' Chesnie queried, not at all with him.

'While I accept that any marriage between us would be for my benefit alone, I hope you'd allow me the same pride.'

She stared at him, mystified. 'I've lost you,' she confessed.

'Your pride precludes me from having affairs outside of our marriage. May I take it that you intend to be celibate too?'

Oh, grief, she could feel herself going pink again. But she had started this, so she swallowed and answered, 'Er—that seems only fair.' And knew it was crunch-time when his expression went deadly serious.

'You'll marry me, Chesnie?' he asked.

As she saw it, it was too late to back out now. Already she felt committed. 'I've nothing else planned for the next couple of years,' she answered, as evenly as just then she was capable.

He smiled then. 'Thank you,' he said quietly. 'I truly appreciate you doing this for me. Given that we have to give the register office a clear fifteen days' notice of our intention to marry, you've no objection if we get on with it straight away?'

'You don't want a long engagement?'

'That's not my way.'

That was true. See it, do it Davenport. She realised then that, the die cast, she was starting to feel less strung up. 'The sooner we marry, the sooner we can divorce,' she said with a smile. Strangely, Joel did not smile back.

'Right,' he said after some moments. 'Let's get down to practicalities.'

'Right,' she agreed.

But was more than a little taken aback when he said, 'I suppose we'll have to invite our families to the wedding.'

'We can't just get married and then explain it's a convenience thing?' she asked.

'Not a chance!' He blocked that notion before it could go any further. 'We have to keep that between our two selves,' he informed her, but did explain. 'I don't know about your folks, but can you see my father keeping something like that to himself for even two weeks, let alone two years?'

'That's a point,' she had to agree.

But was little short of amazed when Joel revealed, 'Only last night I had a phone call from my mother—she wants to meet you.'

'Your *mother* wants to meet me?' Chesnie echoed disbelievingly.

'She returned home yesterday from holidaying abroad. My father lost no time in contacting her to tell her I'd got myself engaged.'

'I take your point. We can't tell our families the real reason for our marrying,' she agreed. Her family was larger than his, from what she could make out. Who was to say that one of her family, one of her brothers-in-law, wouldn't say something in the wrong ear? 'Did you want me to make the arrangements, or shall I leave it with you?'

'You'll have to come to the register office with me to give notice of our intention to marry, but I think, brilliant though you are at organisation, the rest of the details you can leave to me,' Joel decided. And, all work done, nothing else to discuss, Chesnie thought she would return to her room.

'If there's nothing else?' she queried, but was already getting up to leave.

'I don't think so,' Joel answered, escorting her to the door. 'Naturally I shall see you have somewhere pleasant to live when we split up. So...'

Chesnie halted in her tracks. 'Sorry?' she questioned, staring up at him. 'I've already got somewhere pleasant to live.'

'You enjoy living there?'

It was small, but she liked it well enough. 'It has everything I need,' she replied.

Joel did not argue, but, while accepting her answer, *his* answer shook her to her roots. 'If that's what you want,' he replied. 'Let me have your landlord's details and I'll see that he gets a cheque.'

'Am I being a little slow here?'

'It goes without saying that your rent for the next two years is down to me,' he enlightened her.

'I beg your pardon?' Chesnie queried, her pride starting

to bristle—though she saw Joel was the one puzzled this time.

'You've just said you'd like to move back to your present address afterwards,' he reminded her.

'I wasn't thinking of moving out *before*!' she let him know in quick time. His response was equally quick.

'Oh, come on! You can't expect everybody to believe we have a normal marriage if we live at separate addresses!'

'I...' she faltered. She should have thought of this; she should have. 'By "everybody" you mean the board?'

He didn't answer; he didn't have to. He just stood there, looking set and determined, and she began to realise that if she wasn't prepared to move into his home with him then they might as well call if off right now. But—she had already said yes, and, while the thought of living in his home with him made her feel more nervous than ever, she loved him. And he deserved that job.

'I hope you've got plenty of room,' she remarked coolly, and turned to face the door.

'Ample,' he replied. He opened the door, but had one last comment to make. 'Chesnie?' he said. She looked up and would have sworn she saw a hint of devilment in his eyes. 'I'll leave you to tell Pomeroy—that the best man won.'

She thought that perhaps she should give Joel a hint of a frosty look. But how in the world could she find any frost when he must see that her lips were twitching at his comment?

'Goodnight,' she bade him, and try as she might she couldn't keep the laughter out of her voice.

His eyes lingered on her unguarded expression. 'Goodnight,' he returned, and Chesnie walked away, knowing then that she loved him more than enough to marry him.

Work went on as usual, with neither of them referring to their impending marriage. Since Joel had said she could safely leave the arrangements to him, she supposed he would organise everything within the next month or two.

It crossed her mind to wonder what would happen in the event that Joel did not get the chairmanship. But that was unthinkable. He was thinking positive; she must think that way too. Anyhow, she had no need to think what the outcome of their marriage would be should the worst happen. Instant divorce was the answer to that one.

'I'm off home now,' she stated, when on Friday evening she had a clear desk and went in to see him.

'Have a good weekend,' he bade her, but then, leaving what he was doing for a few minutes, 'Have you told your family about—us?' he asked, getting up and coming round to her side of the desk.

'Should I?'

He smiled, and she fell deeper in love with him. 'I think you should.'

She smiled back. 'Then I will.'

'This weekend?' he suggested.

It was his way, she knew, not to delay. 'There are some things you can't do over the telephone—I'll take a drive to Cambridge on Sunday,' she said.

And felt her heartbeats go into overdrive when Joel thought for a moment and then offered, 'I can make myself available Sunday afternoon, if you'd like me to come with you.'

'I…' Oh, yes, she'd love to spend a few hours with him away from the office on Sunday. 'That's all right. Thank you anyway.' She denied herself that pleasure. Goodness, this wasn't going to be your normal kind of marriage. Besides, he had better things to do than spend his time listening to her parents looking for an opening to have a go at one another.

He accepted her decision without comment, but while she was already regretting having deprived herself of his company he was going on, 'I take it you've informed Pomeroy of our marriage plans?'

'I'm having dinner with him tomorrow,' she answered openly—and was quite unprepared for the look of instant displeasure that came over Joel's face.

'The devil you are!' he grated harshly, and, in the same fierce tone, 'You haven't told him yet?'

'I haven't had much chance!' she erupted. And, beating him to it when he looked meaningfully to the telephone, 'As I have already said, there are some things you can't do over the phone.'

'He means that much to you?'

'We're—friends.'

Joel stared down at her. 'And he's in love with you—and has asked you to marry him.'

What could she answer? Love Joel she might, but to her way of thinking it didn't seem right to discuss Philip's emotions this way. Chesnie recognised that her normal cool exterior had a very large dent in it, but she did her very best to show Joel an unflustered façade.

'I'll see you on Monday,' she said, and started to turn away.

'Goodnight,' Joel replied, accepting that she didn't wish to discuss Philip, but giving her a hard look that seemed to say that *he* did the dismissing here.

Chesnie spent Saturday morning doing her usual household chores and not looking forward to seeing Philip that night. She knew it would be the last time she would see him, and that he would be hurt. And she liked him and did not want to hurt him. But there was no alternative.

Philip was due to call at seven, and at four she decided to have a wallow in her bath and try and think up the most tactful and painless way of telling him what she must. She shampooed her hair while she was about it, rinsing off the shampoo with the shower attachment.

Barely had she stepped out of the bath, though, when the outer buzzer went. Who? Nerissa? Hastily Chesnie pulled on her cotton wrap and mopped at her wet hair with a towel as she went. She had wanted to tell Nerissa of her marriage plans first, but realised her parents would feel slighted if they weren't the first to know. But if it were Nerissa at the door, then what would be more natural than that she wouldn't be able to keep her news to herself?

'Hello?' she said into the intercom, her voice welcoming.

'Who were you expecting?' Joel asked bluntly.

Joel? A few weeks ago she might have answered, Obviously not you—but she loved the man. 'I thought it might be one of my sisters,' she answered truthfully, and had nothing more to add.

'Can I see you?' Joel asked when a few seconds had ticked by and she had done nothing about releasing the door catch.

'I—er—I've only just got out of the bath,' she answered in a rush. For goodness' sake—what had happened to sophisticated? Chesnie struggled hard to recapture her image. 'I'm not fit to be seen.'

'I don't believe that for a minute,' Joel replied, and added, 'I know you've an appointment this evening. I won't stay long.'

She wished he would state what he wanted from where he was, on her doorstep, but she had seen his tenacity in action. If he wanted to see her about some small matter then see her he would, though she hadn't a clue what that matter could possibly be.

Without saying another word she activated the door release button, then hared back to the bathroom. She wasted valuable time trying to dry her hair, then realised she had other priorities and wound a towel around it. She was in the middle of making her thin wrap more secure when Joel rang the doorbell.

She would at least have liked to put some underwear on, but there was no time. Joel had said he wouldn't stay long. He was right there. She was going to send him on his way the minute he'd told her the reason for his call.

'Come in,' she greeted him on opening the door, her

heart going all wobbly again. He seemed taller somehow in his casual clothes.

He followed her in to her sitting room, but when she might have suggested he take a seat she bit it back. She was aware of his eyes going over her, just knew that he knew she hadn't a stitch on beneath her thin wrap, and wished, quite desperately, that she had kept him waiting while she put some clothes on. Her light garment was doing little to conceal her curvy contours.

'I really should be getting dressed,' she mumbled, half in apology for the sketch she knew she must look, half as a hint that he should spit out what he'd come to say and leave.

'You look beautiful as you are,' he observed. And, to her astonishment, he seemed to be teasing her, or maybe noticing that she felt awkward and attempting to make her feel more at ease. 'You should wear a pastel-shaded towel around your head more often.'

He was charming her! That was all he had to say and she was ready to wilt! But this would never do. 'As you know, I'm out this evening. But if you've brought me some work you urgently require, I could probably manage it when I come home,' she offered, her tone coolly professional.

Only he did it again. He smiled. And her insides acted all giddy again. 'Am I such a hard task master?' he asked in surprise. Then realised that he probably was. 'Don't answer that,' he ordered, and, putting a hand in his pocket, said, 'I brought you this,' and pulled out a ring box.

'What…?'

'I thought, with everybody knowing we're engaged, you'd better have a ring,' he remarked matter-of-factly, and opened the box to reveal the most exquisite single-stoned engagement ring.

'Joel, I…!' she gasped.

'An emerald, to match your eyes,' he stated, just as matter-of-factly.

'You've...' She was still in shock. He was trying to sound as though he hadn't given it any thought. But surely to have purchased an emerald because of the colour of her eyes must mean he had given it a little thought?

'If it fits you could wear it when you go to Cambridge tomorrow,' he suggested. 'Come to think of it, you might as well start wearing it now.'

'It's lovely,' she murmured, but felt too shy to take it from its box and put it on.

Which made her glad when Joel took the ring out of the box for her. 'Which finger?' he asked, when she was certain he full well knew. She gave him a speaking look, but felt all trembly inside when he caught a hold of her left hand and slid the ring home on the correct finger.

'It fits perfectly!' she whispered, and glanced up to see that he was looking gently at her.

'I'd give you a kiss in the time-honoured manner, only I'm terrified you'd resign.'

Was he teasing again, to get her over any stray touch of awkwardness? She rather thought he was. And liked him more with each new and kind facet she learned of him. 'I'm glad you remembered,' she murmured, but suddenly became conscious that her cotton wrap had stated to gape, revealing more of her right breast than she cared to have on public view. 'Ooh!' she cried on a faint strangled sound, and saw as she went to hurriedly cover herself up that all she had succeeded in doing was drawing Joel's attention to her person. Being taller, he had quite a good view, she knew.

She saw him grin as he dragged his gaze back from the creamy silken swell of her breast. 'Er—don't catch cold,' he commented humorously, and was still grinning as he added, 'I'll see myself out.'

Chesnie was left staring after him. She heard the door close, and collapsed into a chair. Then found she was gazing at the ring on her finger. It was absolutely gorgeous, but she could hardly believe how it had got there. Or indeed, for that matter, that Joel had purchased it and had brought it to her at all.

How long she sat there just looking at the engagement ring, just looking and thinking of how Joel had adopted a teasing manner when he had seen that she felt awkward, Chesnie could not have said. Only when it came to her that she had better start doing something about her hair if she didn't want to look a sight when Philip called for her did she move.

She couldn't resist another glance to her ring, though. But it was then, as she recalled Joel's 'you might as well start wearing it now' that she realised she could not. She had to tell Philip first, and it just seemed a bit—well, not quite nice to be sporting Joel's ring when she told Philip.

Suddenly, thinking of that remark Joel had made, she found she was wondering if Joel had *wanted* her to wear his ring that night. Was he in fact—staking his claim, so to speak? Rot, said her head. As if.

Philip seemed in a serious frame of mind when, just before seven that evening, he called for her. She didn't invite him up to her flat but went straight down, wanting to get said what she had to say while at the same time not wanting to hurt Philip.

But, as things turned out, he already knew. She went with him to his car, but instead of setting the car in motion, as she expected, Philip turned to her and said in a rush, 'I've heard that you and Davenport are an item.'

Chesnie was amazed. 'How did...?' she gasped. Even with the evidence she had that business news travelled fast, she was absolutely stunned that this personal matter had reached him.

'It's true, then?' he questioned, hope fading from his eyes.

'I'm sorry, Philip. I really am,' she apologised. 'I wanted to tell you myself. I intended to...'

'You were going to tell me tonight that this is our last

date?' he asked, and Chesnie could see no way of easing what seemed painful for him.

She offered to cancel their dinner date, but Philip would not hear of it. But the evening was not a success, and when Philip took her home she did not resist when he took her in his arms and held her close for some moments before at last he kissed her.

'Goodbye, darling,' he said.

And Chesnie went up to her flat, feeling near to tears that she had hurt him but aware that she and Philip would never be anything more than the friends she had told Joel they were. When Philip had held her in his arms just now she had felt only sorrow. Joel had only to touch her hand, as he had that afternoon when he had put his ring on her finger, and she tingled all over, felt alive and aware.

Her parents were staggered when, the next day, she told them that she was engaged to be married. 'Why isn't he with you?' her mother asked, getting over her shock.

'Joel wanted to come,' Chesnie began to explain—though 'wanted' was putting it a bit strongly, she knew. 'But he's extremely busy.' That didn't go down too well, and Chesnie found herself inventing. 'We've decided to marry quite soon, so he's rushing to clear away as much as he can so we can spend more time together.'

'I hope you're going to give me enough notice so I can get myself a new outfit!' was her mother's only comment, and Chesnie saw that Joel had been right when he had said they would have to invite their two families to the wedding. Her mother was talking about what she would wear and she hadn't been invited yet!

Chesnie phoned her sisters from her parents' home, and found it little short of amazing that, when her sisters' marriages were such strife-torn disasters, they should be overjoyed at her news. 'Oh, how wonderful!' Nerissa sighed.

Robina was in raptures. 'You dark horse—you said you'd never marry. I couldn't be more pleased!' she enthused.

'Where have you been hiding him?' squealed Tonia excitedly. 'I'm so happy for you.'

Chesnie went into work on Monday still feeling bemused by her family's reaction. 'Good morning,' she bade her fiancé formally, and went all squashy inside when he did her the courtesy of leaving his desk and coming through to her office to see her.

'Any problems?' he enquired, his eyes taking in her neat, trim shape in the sage-green suit.

By 'any problems' she guessed he meant had she told her parents and Philip? 'I've told everyone who needs to be told,' she answered.

He nodded, then said pleasantly, 'I'm glad you're wearing your engagement ring,' and returned to his office. Did the man miss nothing?

Chesnie worked late on Monday, and was busy preparing data on Tuesday morning for a meeting Joel had the next day when he came in to see her. She discovered he had been busy making telephone calls and needed her to go out with him within the next hour.

'I'll have my notepad ready,' she answered, thinking they must be going out on some business matter.

'You won't need it,' he answered, and, when she stared at him uncomprehendingly, 'Have you any plans for two weeks next Saturday?'

'You need me to work?' she asked, ready, willing and able.

'I thought we might get married,' he suggested casually—and she went hot all over. She hadn't been expecting it this soon.

'I—er—I'd better ring my mother. She wants to buy a new outfit,' Chesnie said on a rush of breath, only just holding back a gulp.

But nearly fell off her chair when Joel remarked softly, 'You really are wonderful, aren't you?'

Because she wasn't having forty fits! Thank goodness he didn't know the sudden mass of panic going on inside her.

'I wouldn't dream of arguing with you,' she replied as coolly as she was able.

He gave her a half-smile and then, as practical as ever, 'We need to go to the register office to give notice. We'll need to call at your place first, for either your birth certificate or your passport,' he stated. 'I'm afraid we've a busy time ahead, but I'll find some free time to give you a hand carting your gear over to my place,' he volunteered, and as it struck Chesnie that soon she would be sleeping every night under his roof, so the reality of what was happening hit her with full force.

She was incapable of replying to his offer, so said the only thing she could think of, 'You don't think you should spend what free time you have—living it up?'

'Living it up?'

Oh, crumbs! He was forcing her to explain! 'In view of the fact that very soon you'll be saying goodbye to your— er...'

He was quick on the uptake, and amused with it. 'Loose-living ways?' he supplied.

'Exactly!' she said, and was sinking fast when he laughed.

'Oh, Chezzie Cosgrove,' he said lightly, 'I think you and I will fare very well together.'

Chezzie! She liked it—but then, she was falling apart. She loved him with all her heart, and—oh, help—their wedding day established, that day was coming nearer!

CHAPTER SEVEN

WHAT with a heavy workload, and going to spend one weekend with her grandfather and the next weekend at her parents' home—to shop with her mother on the Saturday for the new outfit her mother insisted on having—there didn't seem to be a moment spare for Chesnie to pack up her belongings. It was the Monday before her wedding when she found some spare time in which to start filling her suitcases.

She was glad to be busy—even if it did sometimes seem to her that from the moment she had consented to marry Joel this coming Saturday she had not had a second to draw fresh breath. She did not want to have time to spare, time in which to think about what she was doing.

As well as coping with an overloaded work schedule, and after speaking to her mother on the phone that night, who asked pertinent questions about what her youngest daughter would be wearing, Chesnie decided that if her mother could have a new outfit then so could she.

A hurried lunchtime trawl of the shops on Tuesday and Wednesday produced just the right cream-coloured silk dress and three-quarter-length matching coat. A hunt for hat, bag, shoes and gloves caused her to be late getting back to her office.

'Have a good time?' Joel asked when she eventually made it back, spying through the open door the expensive-looking large carriers and other large parcels she came in with.

Chesnie put her shopping down and went into his office, and had to smile as she asked, 'What are you getting married in?'

112

'Heaven help us!' he exclaimed. 'You're not expecting me to do the morning suit bit, are you?'

Chesnie savoured the moment, an imp of mischief unexpectedly taking her. 'Would you?' she asked.

Joel stared into her lovely green eyes which, for all she was straight-faced, could not hide their mischievous sparkle. For long moments he just studied her, before confirming, 'If I have to.'

She laughed lightly, was unable to suppress it. 'An everyday kind of suit will do,' she said, and, aware of his eyes on her, decided enough of this levity—she was going to be working late again tonight, and there were more things to pack when she finally got home.

On Thursday Joel paused in the middle of dictating a letter to enquire, 'Everything going smoothly your end?' which surprised her. Work was work; personal was personal—and never the twain should meet.

'You mean the wedding?'

He paused, staring at her for some moments—a habit he seemed to have got into just recently, she suddenly realised. 'Our wedding,' he said succinctly.

'Oh, well, if you're going to be personal about it,' she said—and, spontaneously, they both burst out laughing.

It was a good moment, the memory of which Chesnie knew she would keep with her for some time. Then Joel was serious as he remarked, 'In the unlikely event there is a problem you need help with—what are fiancés for?'

Her heart did a little flip and she acknowledged that she loved it that he should term himself her fiancé. Her heart did another little flip when, on the heels of that, it came to her that from Saturday on he would be able to term himself her husband.

She had envisaged no such problems. Then on Friday, when she took a breather from work to ring her grandfather to double-check that he would be there at her wedding, one unforeseen problem cropped up. 'I—um—may be a little late,' he confessed.

He was never late! He could not bear unpunctuality in any shape! 'What's wrong?' Chesnie was just asking, when Joel came in, saw she was on the phone—but decided to wait.

'Nothing's wrong,' Rufus Cosgrove assured her.

'Yes, there is,' Chesnie responded quietly. 'Come on, Gramps,' she prised gently, but determinedly, 'tell me what's happened.'

Reluctantly, over the next minute or so, he revealed that he had only just heard that there were going to be weekend rail disruptions while track maintenance was being carried out, which would affect the route he intended to travel on. 'But I'll get there as soon as I can,' he ended cheerfully.

Chesnie said goodbye to him and put the phone down, her mind busy. 'A trouble shared?' Joel interrupted her thoughts.

She smiled at him. She'd been rushed off her feet, but for all that she had just spent a most pleasant week working with him. 'It's not trouble, exactly,' she answered. 'Though, on thinking about it, I'll have to put off bringing my stuff over to you until—er—tomorrow.'

'Tomorrow?' He seemed surprised. 'You *have* remembered you're getting married tomorrow?'

'Of course I have,' she replied, starting to feel heated. For pity's sake! On account of tomorrow she'd chased around like a scalded cat all this week!

Joel was still looking. 'So why are we altering our plans for this evening?' he wanted to know.

'I need to drive to Herefordshire tonight,' she answered.

'Because?'

Chesnie looked back at him, then had to concede that, albeit this was nothing to do with work, it was possibly a little something to do with Joel after all. 'Because there's weekend disruption of the rail service on my grandfather's route, and I'm afraid he might not be able to make it to the register office in time for the ceremony tomorrow, and—' She broke off—and started to feel angry with Joel

Davenport and his dogged tenacity when he wanted more than that.

'And?' he insisted.

'And,' she erupted, feeling self-conscious and blaming him for it, 'I want him to be there. I know it's irrational, that ours will not be the usual kind of marriage, but—but he's special to me, and—and,' she ended stubbornly, 'and I want him there.'

She felt stupid, but wouldn't back down, and stared solemnly, stubbornly, at Joel. He stared back, then quietly assured her, 'Then you shall have him there.' With which he strolled back to his office and closed the door. A few minutes later he was coming back to suggest, 'You might like to let your grandfather know that one of our drivers will pick him up at nine tomorrow morning.'

Chesnie looked at him open-mouthed. 'B...'

'That should get him here in ample time to see you married,' Joel stated. 'The same driver will take him back when your grandfather's ready.' And, when she continued to look at him absolutely dumbfounded, 'What's the matter?' he asked. 'You think you're the only one who can solve problems?'

She didn't, of course, but had to smile, and felt the need to explain. 'I'm sorry to have to bother anyone. Normally my grandfather would drive himself, only...'

'Only you've got his car.'

This man she was marrying forgot nothing! 'I'll be giving it back to him as soon as he moves into the cottage he's just bought,' she said. Then, realising Joel probably had more work to do than she had, she felt she had said enough on the subject, and added simply, 'Thank you, Joel.'

He paused only to instruct, 'Don't forget to let the motor section have your grandfather's present address.' And on his way to his own office tossed over his shoulder, 'Your favourite baggage-handler will call at your place tonight— as planned.'

Chesnie carried on working but suddenly became aware that she was working with a ridiculous smile on her face. Good heavens! Though, on thinking about it, for all she had been working in overdrive for most of the time, that smile had had a great number of airings recently. And, come to think of it, having worked for Joel for around five months now, never had she known him so light-hearted as he had been all this week either. Though in his case he was light-hearted because after tomorrow his battle for the chairmanship would be a little more cemented in his favour. So why was she smiling? Perish the thought that it was because she was marrying the man.

At half past four the door opened and Joel came into her office. The present chairman was with him and was carrying the most wonderful bouquet of flowers.

'Joel tells me you both wish to marry without any fuss, but I couldn't let this occasion pass without coming to wish you the very best of everything.' Winslow Yeatman beamed.

Chesnie had been standing, about to do some filing. She put down her papers and came away from the filing cabinet. 'Thank you,' she said as she smiled and accepted the bouquet.

'I've told Winslow our wedding is to be a family-only affair. But we'll be having a party to celebrate later in the year—won't we, darling?' Joel commented, coming over and setting her pulses jumping by placing an arm about her shoulders.

'Be sure Flora and I get an invite.' Winslow beamed again, and Chesnie, finding the idea of entertaining him and who knew who else quite terrifying, continued to smile too.

'Of course,' she assured him, and chatted with him for a few minutes before he and Joel went into Joel's office.

Chesnie got on with her filing, and only then, her filing requiring no great feat of brain-power, did it start to dawn on her that there was likely to be more to this marriage than merely speaking her vows tomorrow.

Though as she began to get used to the notion of being hostess at a party to which all of the 'big-wigs' of Yeatman Trading would be invited, so her initial reaction of being terrified at the very idea began to fade. Should Joel have been serious then, nerve-racking though it would probably be, Chesnie knew—perhaps with a few tips from Nerissa, who was used to entertaining big-time—that she would cope.

She left her office as Miss Cosgrove at six-thirty, and drove home finding she was again smiling as she mused that on Monday she would return as Mrs Davenport. She abruptly stopped smiling. She didn't want to marry—ever. Well, that was— Oh, hang it—roll on tomorrow. Let's get it over and done with.

Strangely, when Chesnie was forever going in to Joel's office to see him, and had only parted from him a couple of hours ago, she experienced a feeling of shyness when he called at her flat that night. She covered her shyness with her calm, efficient PA manner as she invited him in.

'What happened in between our last goodbye and now?' Joel wanted to know, clearly remembering, as did she, their amicable parting when she'd left the office.

'I'm sorry,' she apologised, and wanted to leave it there—but then found that when you loved someone it wasn't that easy to be detached, and that there was a tendency to want to meet them halfway. 'I…' She hesitated, then plumped for the truth. 'I can hardly believe it—and you'll think I'm being ridiculous—but I think I'm feeling shy.'

Joel stared at her. 'Of me?' he asked, and then his mouth, his superb mouth, started to curve upwards. 'It's a new situation for both of us,' he said softly. 'But as long as you're not about to change your mind we'll be fine,' he promised and, making her heart thunder, he ran the back of his hand down the side of her face. Then, his manner changing to his usual one of 'let's get things done', 'Shall we get your belongings over to my place?'

His place was a very different place from hers. It was in a better area, for a start. It was modern and in a relatively new building. The rooms were large and had carpets you could hide your ankles in, and beautiful furniture with clean-cut lines.

Joel showed her over the whole of the apartment, opening the door to his bedroom to show her the layout of everywhere, as though to endorse that she would not be any casual visitor. Saying, in effect, she realised with a glow of warmth, that she must feel that his home was her home too.

'I thought you'd like to have this bedroom,' he said, leading the way to a bedroom with its own adjoining bathroom, which was just across the hall from his. 'Feel free to change anything that doesn't please your eye. If you'd prefer a different set of furniture…'

'It's lovely as it is,' she said, and couldn't fault the spacious room and its abundant wardrobe space.

They went into the kitchen, where he offered to make her coffee, but she had started to feel shy again—though didn't make the mistake of adopting her PA cover this time.

'I think I'd better go home,' she said lightly, beginning to feel a little churned up when she thought of how, from tomorrow and for the next two years, her home would be here—with Joel. 'Er—who keeps your home looking so lovely?' she asked, to cover her shaky feelings.

'A very kind fairy by the name of Mrs Attwood. She arrives several times a week, cleans, sometimes cooks, shops. I just leave her a note. Very often I don't see her for months on end.' He looked pleasantly over to Chesnie and she somehow knew that he had seen her shyness and was answering her question in detail to help her get over her shy moment. She fell yet deeper in love with him.

It was getting on for eleven when he drew his car up outside of her flat. She was feeling all right with him again. Indeed she felt comfortable with him, and, not wanting to be left alone to have last-minute doubts about the wisdom of what she was doing, would have liked to invite him up for coffee. But, regardless of the fact that she was marrying him tomorrow, theirs wasn't that sort of casual relationship. So she got out of the car without a word, and Joel came to the outside door with her.

'Your sister's driving you to the register office, isn't she?' he asked before he let her go, confirming there were no last-minute snags.

'Nerissa insists,' Chesnie replied.

'Until tomorrow, then,' he said, and went. And Chesnie wanted him back. Suddenly there were a dozen or more matters she wanted to discuss with him.

What did they do after the ceremony, for instance, after they'd finished eating and their families had gone their separate ways? Did she go back to his apartment, change and take herself off to the cinema? Go go-cart racing? Shopping? Did he shrug his shoulders and shut himself away somewhere with a good book? And what about meal times? She should have asked. Did she make herself a sandwich and eat it in the kitchen while he dined on some delicacy Mrs Attwood had cooked?

Chesnie did not sleep well, and was wide awake long before her alarm clock sounded. Nerissa rang at eight. 'Are you in a stew?' she asked lightly.

Chesnie had thought her years of training herself to be composed would see her scorning any such idea. But, 'In a word, yes,' she replied. She knew that she would go through with it, she had promised, but oh, how she wished it all over and done with.

'I'll come round early,' Nerissa promised. She had previously blithely stated that her husband was big enough to find his own way to the register office, and that she would meet him there.

True to her word, Nerissa arrived with ample time to spare. 'Coffee?' Chesnie offered.

'I'll make it. You're supposed to be waited on today.'

They were sitting sipping coffee when Nerissa enquired, 'Anything in particular bothering you?'

Where to start? Chesnie shook her head. 'I just didn't expect to feel this—jittery.'

'Par for the course,' Nerissa said with a smile. 'You'll be fine once you see Joel again.'

She was right, Chesnie discovered when she and Nerissa entered the register office. Joel was already there, and was in conversation with her family, a tall, aristocratic woman whom Chesnie took to be his mother, and Magnus. Joel was wearing a smart suit she hadn't seen before, and immediately he saw her he excused himself and came over. Nerissa wandered over to her husband.

'You're not keeping me waiting!' Joel greeted her with a smile, and, taking both her hands in his, he bent and kissed her cheek. She should have been ready for it—it would have looked more odd if he *hadn't* saluted her that way—but she jerked away.

'Sorry,' she immediately whispered.

He bent close to her ear. 'Don't be nervous,' he instructed softly. 'Everything's going to work out well.' He pulled back, an admiring look in his eyes as he surveyed her in her cream silk outfit. 'And you look totally exquisite.' He smiled at her—and suddenly she was feeling better. 'I've introduced myself to your family. When you've said hello to them you must come and say hello to mine.'

Chesnie *knew* she was a bride, but only when one by one her family embraced and kissed her did she actually begin to feel like one. She had been afraid that perhaps she had gone over the top with her outfit. But seeing not only her family but Joel's mother arrayed in wedding finery made her realise she would have looked very much the poor relation had she not bothered.

She introduced Joel to Nerissa and, since her grandfather wasn't one to push himself forwards, Chesnie went and gave him a special hug. In turn she was given a big hug by Magnus Davenport. 'I've always wanted a daughter,' he asserted, with a sly look at his ex-wife. She ignored him.

'Chesnie,' Dorothea Davenport greeted her warmly when Joel introduced her. 'I'm so glad to meet you at last.' She did not embrace or kiss Chesnie, as everyone else had, and shortly afterwards Chesnie and Joel were called to see the registrar.

The ceremony passed in something of a haze for Chesnie. She made her responses when called upon to do so, felt Joel take a hold of her hand to slide a gold band on her wedding finger, and knew that her inner trembling had communicated itself to him when, for the briefest moment, he paused. Then he looked into her eyes and smiled the most wonderful smile.

She was his wife! For someone who had never wanted to be married, Chesnie had to admit, she didn't feel so bad. And Joel didn't look too upset to have given up his freedom either, she noted, as briefly he touched his lips to hers. 'Thank you,' he said quietly—and she was drowning!

'Any time,' she replied, and they looked into each other's eyes—and laughed.

Then, while his parents were congratulating him, her family were crowding round to add their good wishes. As they went on to congratulate Joel, Chesnie had a moment or two alone with her grandfather.

'Promise me you'll be happy,' he said, and Chesnie knew then why, apart from her love for him, it had been important to her that her grandfather was there. Of all her family, his was the only marriage that had been wonderful. She had somehow needed to know on this day that not all the Cosgrove marriages ended in disaster.

'I will be, Gramps,' she assured him.

'I couldn't bear it if I thought you'd end up like your sisters.'

Oh, Gramps. Guilt smote her. His marriage to her grandmother had been near perfect. Gramps wanted the same for her. She loved him so much she felt then that she wanted to confess everything to him. But, conversely, she loved him too much to want to cause him a moment's distress. So she smiled and kissed his worn cheek and laughed as she replied, 'Didn't you know? I'm different.'

'I'm banking on it,' he laughed back. Then Dorothea Davenport had come to stand ready to offer her good wishes. And over the next few minutes, when Dorothea Davenport did give her a kiss of congratulation, Chesnie started to like Joel's mother.

Especially when, with a quick look to check that her ex-husband wasn't within earshot, she confided, 'Don't tell Magnus, but I've always wanted a daughter too,' adding, 'Where is Magnus, by the way? The last time I saw him he was conning your sister—Nerissa, isn't it?—into taking him to lunch one day next week.'

They were having a quiet smile about it when Joel came over to them, closely followed by Magnus. 'I know you and Joel are going to be happy together,' Magnus said, kissing Chesnie's cheek. 'You're not like any of those other women he—'

'Thank you, Father,' Joel interrupted him. 'I'm not sure Chesnie is interested.'

'Sorry,' Magnus apologised with a grin. 'Though you can't expect to have any secrets where families are concerned. Have 'em all together and somebody's bound to end up embarrassed.'

As was proved when, after adjourning to a smart hotel where Joel had organised a private luncheon, they were mid-way through the celebratory meal and Chesnie's mother, after recharging her bickering batteries by having a stab at her husband, turned to Magnus to impart, 'I always knew Chesnie would marry someone she works with. She's always been much too busy to go out looking for someone.'

And if that wasn't embarrassing enough—'go out looking for someone'—as if ensnaring some man was the be-all and end-all of existence—Chesnie's sister Tonia, probably trying to make things better, chimed in with, 'You're the only one of us who ever thought Chesnie would marry at all, Mother. She's always sworn that she would never say ''I do'' to any man.'

'That was before the love-bug crept up on her unexpectedly.' Her sister Robina chipped in with her two pennyworth—and Chesnie was aware that Joel, sitting next to her, was looking at her.

'You've gone a touch pink,' he murmured in an undertone.

'Your father was right!' she replied, glancing at him, and felt quite spell-bound when he grinned handsomely.

Had she imagined that she might feel awkward once the wedding party ended and she was left alone with Joel, she soon realised that she need not have worried. Following tradition, and after more hugs and kisses to speed them on their way, she and Joel were the first to leave.

'Anything in particular you'd like to do this afternoon?' he surprised her by asking as they drove away from the hotel.

'I—er—thought, as soon as I've changed, that I'd better get on with my unpacking,' she replied, the notion to sort out her belongings only then coming to her.

'We can eat in or out—whichever you prefer,' he suggested, laying to rest any idea she might have nursed that it might be 'I do solemnly declare...' at the register office and then, I'll see you at the office come Monday.

'In, I think,' Chesnie opted. 'Though I don't think I shall be ready for another meal for a while.'

Chesnie wasn't at all sure how they would fare living under the same roof, and she suddenly realised that Joel might initially be experiencing similar slightly awkward feelings as she was, in the circumstance of their starting to live together under the same roof. That realisation tempered her own anxious feelings, so that by the time he had garaged his car and they were inside his apartment she was more than ready to meet him halfway.

With the intention of going straight to her room, she set

off along the hall. Only to halt and to turn when Joel called, 'Chesnie!' She took a couple of steps back towards him. Joel came nearer, and stopped to look down into her eyes. 'Thank you for today,' he said quietly. 'It means a great deal to me.'

'I know,' she answered softly, her mood all-giving.

'Is there anything I can do for you in return?' he asked, and she knew, proud man that he was, that she would only have to mention it, whatever 'it' might be, and it would be done. But then he said something that caused *her* pride to shoot off into orbit. 'Naturally I'll arrange for an allowance to be paid into your bank acc—'

'I don't want an allowance!' she exploded, offended on the instant.

'Don't be ridiculous!' he retorted crisply, his easy manner gone. 'You're married now. You're my wife. Of course you—'

'I didn't marry you for your money!' she erupted hotly.

'I know *that*!' he stated tersely. Then caused her anger to depart as swiftly as it had arrived, panic taking its place, when he paused and, his stern expression fading, asked, 'Just why *did* you marry me, Chesnie?'

Oh, heaven help us! Suddenly she was desperate to keep this sharp and clever man from guessing that, had she not fallen heart and soul in love with him, it was very doubtful she would have married him at all. 'Given that you must have caught me at a weak moment, what PA worthy of the name could resist the chance to be PA to the chairman?' she found from a barren nowhere.

He must have accepted that, she realised, because though she had seen him question, question and question that which he needed to know, he did not pursue it, and suddenly the corners of his mouth were turning upwards. Then his glance went to her mouth and, unhurriedly, his hands were reaching for her and he was giving her heart failure by drawing her to him. 'I really do think, Mrs Davenport,' he began as, unresisting, slightly mesmerised, she went into the circle of his arms, 'that we should seal today's events with a kiss of marriage.'

She stared at him, but as his lips met hers she closed her eyes. With her heart banging against her ribs she thrilled to the feel of his firm arms about her as warmly he kissed her. As kisses went, it started as a fairly chaste kiss, but his arms tightened about her and his kiss deepened, and Chesnie was quite unprepared for the less than chaste re-action of her body. She had never been up this close to him before, but the feel of the hard muscles of his arms about her, the feel of his body against hers, the feel of his body warmth, was staggering. She loved the feel of him, loved his touch, and held on to him—because she had to. She was under the spell of him, mindless of anything save him and his wonderful mouth over hers as she responded to his kiss.

Only when he broke his kiss and took a step back, his body no longer touching her, was Chesnie able to regain a little brain-power. 'Oh, by the way,' she said, from a cool, off-hand heaven-alone-knew-where, considering that her legs were about to buckle, 'I think I left my gloves in your car.'

Joel stared at her in astonishment, and she rather gathered he was used to a very different reaction to his kisses. Then, unexpectedly, he burst out laughing, his eyes alight with amusement, and commented, 'Do you know, Chesnie? I believe I could get to quite enjoy living with you.'

Inside she was smiling. But without a word she turned and walked towards her bedroom. She only hoped her legs would hold up until she got there!

CHAPTER EIGHT

THEY had been married for two weeks when Chesnie became aware that, while not husband and wife except on paper, their relationship seemed to have changed in some subtle way. That change, she realised on thinking about it, had begun when Joel had claimed that kiss of marriage on their wedding day.

She could not have explained what exactly was different, but, while she still performed her duties as his PA in her usual efficient manner, away from the office PA and boss just didn't come into it. Though what their relationship was, apart from on their marriage certificate, she was unsure.

Were they friends? She supposed they might be. Joel was always friendly to her, considerate to her, even, as if believing that her having moved from her own home and into his had been a big adjustment to make.

Not that she saw a great deal of him out of the office. In her view Joel, having lived on his own for a number of years, must also have had to adjust to someone living in his space. To give him as much space as possible she would often take herself off to her room—when her preference would have been to stay where he was.

'You don't have to go, you know,' he'd said only last night when, after a gruelling kind of day, he'd had to attend a business dinner but had then come home earlier than she had expected.

'I—er...' That abominable shyness she had become acquainted with recently arrived again to trip her up. 'I—er—quite enjoy my own company,' she'd answered.

'In other words, you've seen quite enough of me for one day?' he'd suggested.

He had sounded a touch put out—was he looking for a fight? She loved him. She didn't want to fight with him. So she had smiled. 'Goodnight,' she'd said, and had gone to bed.

Now, this bright Saturday morning, she was going to do what she could delay doing no longer. Gramps was moving into his new home on Monday—she really must go looking for a car. Joel always left for the office ages before she did, but in any case, what with him sometimes working away or going off for some business conference or other at the end of the day, cadging a lift with him on a daily basis was a non-starter. She needed her own car.

Chesnie went in to the kitchen to make her breakfast, and found Joel there, just finishing his. 'Good morning,' she bade him cheerfully, so truly pleased to see him she forgot all about the cool demeanour she usually showed him. Though, come to think of it, that cool demeanour had slipped quite a bit just lately. But, she excused, why not? He was, after all, family.

'You sound as if you slept well,' he observed lightly.

'That bed is bliss.' Her heart was acting the giddy-goat again. 'Would you like some more coffee?' she asked, going over to the percolator.

'I'll take a cup to my study,' he accepted.

And so the day began. She supposed she could say that they coped with living under the same roof quite well. She went off looking for a new-second-hand car and saw one within her price range but which she was undecided about. She decided to think it over and go and take another look in her lunch hour on Monday.

'Want to do anything in particular tonight?' Joel asked when she returned to the apartment and went into the drawing room.

She looked at him. 'Was I wrong?' she asked.

'Enlighten me?'

'To stipulate no girlfriends?'

He grinned; her heart bumped. 'You're suggesting I must be bored because I want to take my wife out?'

Want to? Wife! She was crazy about him. She laughed. 'I've got this boss who keeps my nose to the grindstone. At weekends all I want to do is just curl up with a book,' she lied, declining his offer to take her somewhere.

She went to her room, already mentally kicking herself for refusing his invitation. Would it have hurt to have enjoyed some more of his company, for goodness' sake? Had she resigned herself to staying in alone reading every weekend for the next two years? Honestly!

Yes, but, if possible, she was falling even deeper in love with him day by day. How would they fare if he saw her love for him? He'd be embarrassed—she'd be *mortified*. Already her guard had slipped so much as to be almost permanently down. In the office she could mask her feelings—at home, witnessing at first hand a less businesslike, more lenient side to Joel, she greatly feared lest he gained an inkling of her caring for him.

On Sunday morning the phone rang while Joel was in his study. When he didn't answer the phone straight away she presumed he was tied up with work, so took the call. It was Magnus. He said he hadn't rung to speak with Joel especially, but said he was lonely.

Joel was just emerging from his study when she got back from the supermarket. 'We ran out of something?' he enquired, his glance on the three plastic carriers in her hands.

'I—um—invited your father to lunch,' she said in a rush—and saw Joel's look of amusement.

'You mean he rang, gave you some sob story, and you fell for it.' He immediately saw how it had been.

'You're invited too, if you like,' she offered in a take-it-or-leave-it fashion.

'A home-cooked meal that didn't come out of the freezer—try to keep me away.'

It was a good time that Sunday lunchtime. One Chesnie knew she would ever remember. For all Joel had no illusions about his father, he treated him with all the respect due not only to his parent, but also to someone whom his wife had invited into their home—and she loved Joel for it.

But Monday was work again and busy, busy, busy, with an unexpected need arising for her to make arrangements to fly with Joel tomorrow to their offices in Glasgow. Chesnie was so absorbed she didn't even have time to think of going to take a second look at the car she was considering buying, much less take a lunch hour to go and look at it.

On Tuesday she went to the airport with Joel in his car. They talked about work some of the way, and shared some business papers during the flight, and she felt so much part and parcel of the whole venture that she never wanted to work anywhere else.

Though, having been calm when they arrived at their hotel, Chesnie's composure was shattered when, in relation to the booking she had made, the male receptionist smilingly went to hand her the key to her room—and Joel stopped him.

Both Chesnie and the receptionist shot him a startled look. Joel was not one whit put out of countenance. 'Miss Cosgrove must have forgotten,' he said, turning to her but addressing the desk clerk. 'We were married two weeks ago.' And, turning back to the clerk, 'Mrs Davenport will be sharing the suite with me.'

Instantly Chesnie called on her reserves to hide her inner feelings, and smiled her guarded smile while the man congratulated Joel. But she wasn't feeling at all kindly disposed towards the man she had married when she rode up in the lift with him. Other people being in the lift prevented her from letting Joel know exactly how she did feel.

'Why did you do that?' she demanded, once they were in the suite and the door was closed on the outside world.

'What's your problem?' Joel enquired, not a glimmer of a smile about him.

'I'd have been quite comfortable in a room on my own.'

'You'll have a room on your own. There are two bedrooms with this suite,' he explained patiently, as one would to a child. She did not thank him for it. His apartment was large, this suite was largish—but to go away together, to share it, to let the staff know that they were married, made it all seem too intimate somehow. 'And,' Joel went on when she just stared stubbornly at him, 'I don't want word getting back to the board that we don't share.'

'How could it get back?' she demanded to know.

'All it takes is for you to accidentally leave something behind in your single room and the hotel to ring our London office and say where they found it.'

He had her there. She could think of half a dozen scenarios where word could get back to London. 'You think of everything!' she complained in disgust.

'True,' he accepted, and she had to laugh. And, seeing the way her lovely face lit up, he placed an arm about her shoulders, gave her a squeeze and said, 'Come on, flower, we're going to be late.'

She dropped her overnight bag where she stood and went with him to the meeting, the short car ride giving her very little time in which to get her accustomed composure back together. Flower? That squeeze of her shoulders which, if she hadn't know better, she might have confused with a hug of affection?

From the moment they entered the meeting it was notepad out and concentrate, so that Chesnie didn't have a moment in which to think her own thoughts. They had a sandwich at lunchtime, and worked on. But when at five Joel suggested that, because of some data he wanted typed back for the morning, she might like to return to the hotel, she took her leave. Joel stayed behind, and the drive back to the hotel gave her a chance to savour again the more pleasant part of their spat that morning.

She didn't really think that had been a hug of affection, and a squeeze about her shoulders was a million miles away from Joel being even a tiny bit in love with her. But she reckoned, and hoped, that he must at least like her. He trusted her, she knew that—had to. Trust was all part of the sometimes highly confidential work she did for him. Trust? Like? Both, she realised. For, from what she knew of him, she could not see Joel, even for the expediency of getting that chairman's job, marrying himself to someone he didn't like.

On that fairly satisfying thought she reached their hotel, went up to their suite and set up her makeshift office and got on with some work. She had been typing for about an hour when her mind wandered to consider that the first thing Joel would want when he got back would be either a drink or a shower. She wanted a shower too, but there was only one bathroom. If she showered now, it would leave the bathroom free for Joel when he came in.

Abandoning her typing for a short while, Chesnie, using the smaller of the two bedrooms, exchanged the clothes she had worn all day for her cotton wrap and, armed with her bag of toiletries, headed for the shower.

Her hair got wet, so she thought she might as well shampoo it.

Fifteen minutes later she was back in her room and was busy with the hairdryer. She thought that rather than get back into her business gear she might as well change into the smart but casual long skirt and top she had packed.

A dab of moisturiser, a touch of face powder and a smear of lipstick, and she was ready to resume her typing. She was tidy-minded, however, and was putting her room to rights when she realised she had left her toilet bag in the bathroom. She didn't want her belongings cluttering up the bathroom when Joel came in, so went quickly to retrieve it.

It was a fairly large walk-in bathroom and she went boldly in—only to stop dead in her tracks. Joel was already in! In fact he had just stepped out of the bath!

By no chance was she able to adopt a cool front. Stark

naked, Joel turned at the strangled cry that broke from her. And Chesnie, stunned, her face a furious red, started to back away from him, her eyes fixed on his face.

From what her scrambled brain could make out, Joel had not the slightest hang-up about his nakedness, so she could only gather that it was for her benefit that, on seeing her scarlet face, he stretched a hand out for a towel and wrapped it around his waist.

'You're blushing!' he observed, and, a startled look coming to his face, 'You *have* seen a naked man before?'

'I usually close my eyes!' she replied on a hoarse note and, from being too transfixed to move, had never moved so quickly when she did a snappy about-turn and got out of there.

By the time a fully clothed Joel had joined her she had recovered a little of her equilibrium. It was so embarrassing. Well, he hadn't seemed at all flustered, she qualified, but she still felt scarlet right to the tips of her toes.

To his credit he gave her the chance to recover, and didn't mention the incident, but looked over her shoulder at the work she was completing. In silence they worked on. It was a little after eight when Joel announced, 'If I don't get something to eat soon my stomach will think my mouth's on strike.'

He did not suggest that they eat in the suite, as he had before, and she was glad he didn't. While she knew she would have to learn to live with her unfortunate intrusion into his privacy, it was still too fresh—still too intimate.

'I have a key,' he informed her when she picked up the key she had used to gain entry to the suite.

'Fine,' she murmured, realising he must have picked up a spare at Reception when he'd come in. If only he hadn't, if only he'd had to knock on the door for her to let him in, then that bathroom incident never would have happened. As it was she had gone from blocking everything out of her mind to recalling every moment in detail.

She was sitting opposite him in the dining room and they

were mid-way thought their meal when she recalled again what a wonderful body he had. She had seen the back of him first, his broad shoulders, perfect behind and straight legs. Then he had turned and on the instant of panic her eyes had first become riveted on his broad manly chest. Then she had raised her eyes and kept them rigidly on his face.

'Penny for them?' Joel offered for her thoughts.

As though he could read her mind, she went pink. 'They're not worth that much,' she answered lightly, and was glad he let her get away with it. She spoke of any other subject, and tried hard not to think about his chest with that smattering of damp, darkened hair.

Then, 'Why?' he suddenly asked.

Chesnie hadn't a clue what he meant, but somehow felt that it had nothing to do with their work. 'Why not?' she bounced back at him, fearing the worst, fearing that, having given her all the time in the world in which to get herself back together again, he was having a tussle with his curiosity and curiosity had just won.

Then she found that he wasn't taking 'Why not?' for any kind of answer, and, had she thought about it, she supposed she knew enough about him to know that what he wanted to know he always found out.

He tried another tack. 'You don't look frigid.'

'I'm not!' she defended.

'But you've never seen a man minus his clothes before. As naked as—'

'Do you mind? You're blowing my cover!' she exclaimed—rather desperately, it had to be admitted.

Bravely, she met his eyes, but felt all kind of trembly inside when his glance on her suddenly softened. 'I'm embarrassing you—again,' he stated gently. 'I'm sorry,' he apologised. 'You just sort of—surprise me at every turn.' He smiled then, that smile turning into a fantastic grin as he added, 'A man could go a touch crazy in the head about you if he wasn't careful.'

She felt about to swoon. His grin alone was playing havoc with her senses, without that last bit. 'Then you'd better be careful!' From somewhere Chesnie managed to sound as if her backbone was rock-solid, when in actual fact it was meltdown time. 'We part in less than two years, remember?'

'You're not leaving me!' Her eyes shot wide that Joel seemed appalled at the very idea. But, before she could get too thrilled that he appeared extremely loath that she should ever leave him, he added, 'You've proved to be a quite sensational PA,' and again Chesnie was having to make desperate attempts to hide her feelings. It wasn't her, his wife, he was appalled at parting from, but her, his 'quite sensational PA,' he didn't want to lose!

'You have remembered that we're going to end up divorced?' she reminded him.

To her chagrin, he looked relieved. 'I'm counting on it!' he said.

Well, there was more than one way of getting slapped down, she mused. She went to bed that night—and again thought of the way she had seen his splendid uncovered body. She loved him so much, and realised that part of that love was a need to be held by him, to be loved by him, to be made love to by him. But it would never be—so she had better forget such thoughts and concentrate on her career.

She was pleased to return to the London office the next afternoon. Unusually, Joel left the office before she did that night, but when she let herself into what she was now adjusted to being her home, Joel came along the hall to meet her.

'I've something to show you,' he greeted her.

'What...?'

He wouldn't say, but before she could utter another word had taken a hold of her by the arm and was guiding her round the set of garages where she had just parked her grandfather's car for the night.

Joel led her over to one of the garages on the opposite side. 'I've borrowed this one for the week while the owner is touring Wales,' he remarked, and, letting go her arm, he unlocked the garage. Mystified, Chesnie stood there while the garage door rose and disappeared into the roof space. 'What do you think?' he asked, taking hold of her arm again and escorting her inside.

'Very nice,' she replied, realising that he was asking her opinion of what looked like a brand-new top-of-the-range sports car.

'I thought a smaller car would be better for you driving around London and trying to find a parking space,' Joel commented.

Chesnie stared at him in some surprise. 'You want me to drive it?'

'I hope you will. It's yours.'

'*Mine?*' she questioned incredulously. 'B-but...' Words failed her.

'Yours,' Joel confirmed.

'But I can't...'

'You're going to argue. I knew you would. I said to myself, She won't like it. She kicked up a fuss when you wanted to make her an allowance. She's bound to create a fuss over this. Then I thought, Yes, but I really can't let her, the future chairman's wife, be seen driving around in her grandfather's car.' Chesnie stared at him. If she knew anything about Joel she knew without a question of a doubt that he didn't have a snobbish bone in his body. Providing the vehicle was roadworthy, he wouldn't give a hoot what kind of down-market car his wife was seen driving around in. She looked at him speechlessly. 'And what about your poor dear grandfather?' Joel pressed his cause. 'He must be desperate to have his car back.'

What could she do? Joel expected her to argue. She swallowed hard on a knot of pride, hoped she wouldn't have fallen too much in love with the car when the time came when she would have to hand it back, and she smiled.

'Thank you, Joel, it's a beautiful car,' she told him. And, when she knew he hadn't been expecting that at all, she gave him something else he hadn't been expecting either—she stretched up and kissed him.

For a moment his hands gripped her waist and he looked into her eyes. Then they were both stepping away from each other. 'Come on, let me see you put it through its paces,' Joel suggested, and handed her the keys to the car.

Two days later and Chesnie had adjusted to her new car, and was loving it. What she was not loving was the fact that, ever since they had returned from Scotland, she had begun to feel overwhelmed by her feelings for Joel. He was generous to her, kind to her—and she did not seem able to get him out of her head. As a consequence it was taking her all her time to make the concentrated effort needed to hide her feelings for him. Which left her feeling tense and knowing that she had to get away, if only for a few hours, to sort herself out.

She met him in the kitchen at breakfast time on Saturday morning, and knew what she was going to do when, teasingly referring to how she had stated last Saturday that all she wanted to do at the weekends was to curl up with a book, Joel enquired, 'Do you have sufficient reading matter? If not there's an art exhibition we could—'

We! Oh, Joel, don't! There was nothing she would like better than to go with him but—self-preservation won the day. 'I think it's time I returned my grandfather's car,' she butted in.

'You're going to Herefordshire?' Joel was standing by one of the work surfaces and glanced across to where she stood making some toast.

'Gramps moved into his new cottage last Monday. He no longer has a garaging problem.'

'How are you getting back?' Joel wanted to know.

Chesnie thought about that, realising that there was every possibility of weekend rail work still being carried out. 'If I can't make it back today, I'll stay overnight and make an early start on Sunday morning.' She smiled at Joel then, and didn't see why he should be the only one allowed to tease. 'Don't worry. I promise I'll be at my desk for nine sharp on Monday.'

Chesnie, with an overnight bag in her car just in case, was driving out of London when, Joel as ever in her thoughts, she reflected that he had seemed a bit put out that she had turned down his offer of a visit to the art exhibition. Then reality gave her a poke—as if! The only reason Joel was likely to be at all put out was in case his mother or someone rang and began to wonder what was going on that, married for only three weeks, they were so soon spending time apart. But, anyway, Joel could handle that; she knew he could.

Though she had to doubt her own ability on that score when, having been hugged and kissed by her delighted grandfather, his first question was, 'Where's Joel?'

'Joel has some work he needs urgently for Monday,' she replied, hating to lie to her grandfather. But Joel was against anyone knowing the real reason they had married, and he was her first consideration now. So not even to her beloved grandfather could she reveal the secret of her marriage.

Her grandfather was still to a large extent living out of packing cases, and finding homes for his belongings as he used them. Chesnie metaphorically rolled up her sleeves and set to.

After a couple of hours she had cleared many boxes and cartons, but she could still barely move without tripping over something or other.

It had soon become obvious that her grandfather had taken all of his furniture out of storage. It was equally obvious that, hating to part with any of the furniture that had been with him throughout his married life, her grandfather had enough furniture to furnish three cottages, let alone one.

'Your grandmother loved that old dresser,' he said fondly

when Chesnie had just knocked her shin on it, trying to get past.

'It is lovely, Gramps,' Chesnie replied. It was his home; he would decide in due time if he wanted to continue to live in the small sitting room with a large three-piece suite and various other padded chairs. That decision was his and, in her view, no one had the right to make that choice for him.

'How are you getting back?' He suddenly seemed to realise that if she was leaving his car behind she was going to have to use public transport.

Chesnie looked at her surroundings. For all her efforts the place still resembled a dumping ground. And while her heart pulled, wanting to be back with Joel, to be back under Joel's roof, there was just no way she could leave her elderly grandparent to wade through this muddle on his own.

'How about we find homes for all your ornaments and then have a bar meal at the Bull? I'll go back to London in the morning.'

'You'll stay the night?' He looked puzzled.

'*I* thought it was a good idea,' she teased.

'Everything *is* all right with you and Joel, isn't it?' he asked, looking worried. And Chesnie knew then, as she recalled how on her wedding day he had said that he couldn't bear it if he thought her marriage would end up like those of her sisters, that she could not let her grandfather in particular know that there was anything different from what it should be about her marriage.

'Everything's fine!' she answered. 'Joel and I are with each other every day and night.' She managed a light laugh as she added, 'Joel's probably glad to have a few minutes to himself.'

Her grandfather did not look convinced, but managed a smile as he told her she had better go and make up a bed for herself. He would make her a nice cup of tea.

There was barely room to move around in the spare bedroom, more of a junk room, which housed a large double bed, two wardrobes, a dressing table with a chair stacked on top of it, two standard lamps, two boxes of books and other assorted impedimenta. Chesnie wanted to go home. Her heart was aching to go home—to Joel

It was getting on for seven that evening when, having made a great deal of difference to the general cluttered look of the place—she could do nothing about minimising the bulky furniture—Chesnie realised that while she toiled so would her grandfather. Poor sweetheart, he must want a rest.

'Ready for the Bull?' she asked. 'I can finish off the remaining boxes before I leave in the morning.'

She ate her meal wondering what Joel was doing. Was he making himself a meal from the supply of pies and casseroles with which Mrs Attwood regularly stocked up the freezer? Perhaps he intended going out for a meal later. Perhaps... Jealousy took a nip. No, not Joel. He had agreed—no women-friends. Still the same, she could not help but wonder what he would do for relaxation that night. Heaven alone knew he worked hard enough.

It was still relatively early when they left the Bull to walk the short distance back to her grandfather's new home. But as they turned the corner so, with the cottage in view, Chesnie's heart started to beat a crazy rhythm. That car standing outside her grandfather's property looked exactly like...

Joel must have been watching from his rearview mirror for, to make her heart dance a jig, the driver's door all at once opened and, tall, good-looking and, oh, so dear, Joel stepped from the car.

'Joel!' she exclaimed as they neared him, and, strive though she did, she could not keep the smile out of her voice.

'I thought you might be needing a lift back home,' he said, for her grandfather's benefit coming over and lightly kissing her mouth. 'Mr Cosgrove,' he said, turning to hold out his hand to her grandfather.

'You've completed your work earlier than expected,' Rufus Cosgrove commented.

And, still tingling from head to toe from that light kiss, Chesnie could only admire Joel the more that, when he couldn't have a clue what her grandfather was talking about, he smiled as he replied, 'The apartment wasn't the same without Chesnie.'

That pleased her grandfather. 'So you've come to take her home,' he noted, and seemed very happy with that. But he caused Chesnie a few moments' consternation when he suddenly said, 'Chesnie was going to stay the night. Why don't you both stay? Have you anything pressing to get back to London for?'

'Well, no,' Joel admitted, but, as if thinking that Chesnie might want to spend more time with her grandfather, 'I wouldn't want to put you out. I'll check into a hotel somewhere near.'

'Wouldn't hear of it!' Rufus Cosgrove declared stoutly. 'Would we, Chesnie?' He enlisted her support.

She couldn't! Not possibly! It was out of the quest... But—she'd have to! 'Of course Joel must stay with us!' She backed her grandfather firmly—if her insides had just gone to jelly then only she was going to know about it. But, oh, what had she done? But what else could she have done? Gramps mustn't know the truth—he would be devastated! 'Have you eaten?' she asked Joel nicely, as any loving spouse would, her initial panic easing as she pinned her hopes on Joel's brain being sharper than hers just then in this fine mess they were in. He'd find a way of getting them both out of this situation without her grandfather being in the least aware that theirs was not a normal marriage, of that she started to feel certain.

But—no. 'I had something to eat on the way here.' Joel smiled—and had nothing more to add. And while Chesnie had started to panic frantically again—hadn't he realised that this was only a two-bedroomed cottage?—her grandfather was heading for the garden gate.

Once inside the cottage her grandfather was setting about finding Joel a new toothbrush and a pair of pyjamas, while Chesnie was realising that, even if the cottage had boasted three bedrooms, there was no way she and Joel could have occupied separate bedrooms without her grandfather thinking it peculiar.

'The place is a bit of a jumble at the moment,' her grandfather was explaining to Joel, while Chesnie smiled and hid her feeling of going under for the third time.

'You only moved in on Monday,' Joel answered. 'It takes a while to know just where you want to put everything.'

How could he talk so easily, so without stress, so as if the prospect of having to spend a night sleeping in the same room with his platonic wife was neither here nor there to him? She couldn't yet begin to think of him having to sleep in the same bed, let alone the same room. Yet in that over-cluttered room there was barely six inches of floor space free anywhere, and there was nowhere else for him *to* sleep—but in the same bed!

With Joel and her grandfather conversing comfortably, Chesnie began to feel the only stranger here, and went into the kitchen to make a night-time drink. For herself, she'd stay exactly where she was until daylight tomorrow morning, but she doubted her grandfather had ceased his habit of getting up in the middle of the night. No way, Chesnie realised, could she stay down and risk her grandfather coming down to make himself a cup of tea at three tomorrow morning.

'It's been a long day,' her grandfather announced, draining his cup and getting slowly out of his chair.

'It has,' Joel remarked, on his feet too.

Chesnie was loading cups and saucers on to a tray when her grandfather offered, 'I'll show you the facilities and where you'll be sleeping, if you like.'

'You don't mind if I go up first, dear?' Joel asked pleasantly.

Was he serious? She looked at him. His expression was bland—his eyes told a different story. He thinks it's funny!

'I won't be long,' she promised sweetly. Oh, grief! 'I'll just rinse these few things through…'

Won't be long? She knew she could have washed dishes from a seven-course meal—and still wouldn't be ready to climb those stairs. But—oh—what else could she do? With her insides churning she grabbed her overnight bag from beneath the kitchen table—about the only available free space—and climbed the stairs.

She still wasn't ready to join Joel in that bedroom, though. And by no chance was she going to undress in front of him. She ducked into the bathroom and unzipped her bag. From choice she would sleep in her clothes, but didn't fancy her grandfather's comments on her crumpled appearance tomorrow at breakfast.

She showered and changed into her short cotton nightdress and tried desperately hard to be detached. If only she could find some of that calm composure that had seen her deal with many a difficult business situation in the past.

Chesnie shrugged into her cotton wrap, knowing that the difference here was that this was not a business situation. She, who had never slept with a man in her life, was about to now—and she was having kittens about it! And the fact was she was feeling very far removed from being calm and composed.

Only by telling herself that she was not going to sleep with Joel in *that* sense was she able to leave the bathroom. Only by telling herself that Joel was not just anybody, but was someone she knew and liked, was she able to go to the room where she knew he was.

She pushed the door inwards, and her heart sank. She had been hopeful that the light might be out—but it wasn't. She had been hopeful that Joel might be asleep—but he was definitely awake.

Chesnie went in and had never needed her mask of calm efficiency more. She was inwardly shaking like the pro-

verbial leaf. It didn't help a bit to see in that one swift
glance to the bed that Joel had declined the use of her
grandfather's pyjamas—the jacket anyway; she didn't want
to contemplate his trousers. Joel was sitting up in bed and,
daring another glance, she observed he had been reading
one of her grandfather's thrillers. But as Joel politely low-
ered his book she was swamped by the intimacy of spying
his broad hair-roughened chest. Thankfully he was over on
one side of the bed, leaving her ample room on the other.

'Don't stop reading on my account!' Chesnie remarked
as evenly as she was able, and, looking from him and hoping he wasn't looking at her, she quickly disposed of her
wrap and as quickly got into bed. 'I never thought to ask...'
some kind of welcome automaton was taking over '...do
you snore?'

She rather thought the automaton would have carried her
through until she went to sleep—had not Joel laughed. She
could not believe it, but—as though what she'd said had
amused him, as though he found this whole situation funny,
more relaxing than stressful as she was feeling—laugh he
did.

'I've never had any complaints,' he replied lightly, and
she was starting to grow more and more uptight by the
second, sitting there with the bedcovers up to her chin; she
was a while away from even considering lying down.
'You're a cool one,' he commented.

Cool! If only he knew. She dared a sideways glance at
him and, given that he was as near naked as she wanted to
know about, and that her covering was not much better, she
could detect not the smallest hint that Joel might be feeling
inclined to take advantage of the situation.

'I'm sorry,' she apologised, and for the first time since
she had stated 'Of course Joel must stay with us' felt herself
begin to feel less tense. 'I suppose I could have handled all
this differently, only...' She faltered.

'Only?' Joel prompted.

'Only, as I love my grandfather so he loves me, and—

and he sets great store on the institution of marriage. On the day we got married, you and I, he asked me to promise I'd be happy, and said he couldn't bear it if he thought my marriage would turn out to be like those of my sisters.'

'So to protect him, his feelings, you're prepared to sleep the night with me?'

She looked into his eyes to ask, 'Are we friends, Joel?'

He stared into her searching green eyes. And, after long moments of just looking at her, 'I'd like us to be,' he said.

Chesnie smiled a beam of a smile. 'Thank you,' she said simply. 'Gramps will have to know about our divorce, of course, but not for a long time. Eighteen months from now I can start to gently prepare him to hear that you and I will be separating.' With that, she lay down and turned to face the furniture-festooned wall. 'Goodnight,' she said quietly. And waited.

His reply was a long time coming. Then quietly, in return, 'Goodnight, my dear,' he said, and switched off the light.

It took Chesnie an age to get to sleep. My dear? Was that a new habit formed from using an endearment for her grandfather's ears? Did friends share that sort of warm familiarity? Joel had said he would like them to be friends. Her heart leapt. Friends meant he liked her, and, while like wasn't love, she would still want him to be her friend when their marriage was over.

Her thoughts started to become a little woolly. She had an urge to change her position, to turn over, but fear of bumping into Joel made her deny that urge. She started to marvel suddenly that she was sharing a bed with him at all. He could have insisted on going to a hotel, she realised. Though of course this marriage was for Joel's benefit, not hers. Her thoughts became even woollier—but she wouldn't have married him at all had she not loved him. But he was never to know that.

On that thought, sleep claimed her, and in sleep her body gave in to the urge to change her position. In fact, over the following hours she changed her position many times, and each time, as if unconsciously magnet-drawn, Chesnie moved closer to the man she loved.

Dawn was just breaking when Chesnie awakened. She opened her eyes, saw patterned curtains that were not her own, and in split seconds was blasted with memory of where she was, how and why she was there and—whom she was sleeping with! But over and above all that, screaming in, came the realisation that she did not have her head on her pillow. Alarm raking her, she awakened to the fact she had been resting with her head—on Joel's shoulder! Sleeping, incredibly, with his right arm about her.

She gave a small jerk of movement, perhaps intending to leap out of bed—she couldn't be sure—panic taking her that she must have edged towards him during the night and was invading his space.

But—and she was sure she didn't imagine it—that arm about her gave her a small squeeze, as if to say, Stay exactly where you are, and whether or not it *was* her imagination after all, she obeyed.

Joel might be awake, he might be asleep; she couldn't tell. But as she relaxed against him so those few moments of lying there, close to Joel, closer to him than she had ever been, just seemed—beautiful. So beautiful she did not want to move and spoil it.

She felt safe, secure in his hold. She even felt a little loved when, if her imagination wasn't playing dastardly tricks on her, she felt a light pressure on her head—as if Joel had kissed her hair.

Kissed her hair! Don't be ridiculous! Chesnie decided, exquisite though it was to be held so close to him, that she ought to get up. End it now before her imagination got worse.

She went to move—and felt a slight tensing in that arm around her, almost as if Joel too felt that these moments were beautiful and did not want them to end. And, even though a second later she was discounting any such wild fantasy, she no longer seemed to have the will-power to move.

'I...' she murmured on a breathless sound, then found more vocal power, albeit keeping her voice low, just in case Joel was asleep, as she confessed, 'I've never slept with a man before.'

Joel's body seemed to still, and she became certain that he was awake. And knew it for the truth when he quietly asked, 'In—any sense?'

She wanted to look at him, to see his dear face, but was afraid to disturb this wonderful time with him. 'Does that make me odd?'

'It makes me wish you hadn't told me.'

'Why?'

She was sure she could hear laughter in his voice when he answered, 'It makes you—untouchable.'

She felt like laughing too. She loved lying here with him like this—it was like being married. 'That's a rotten thing to say to a wife on a fine Sunday morning,' she replied, quite without thinking—but was relieved when his chest shook and she heard him laugh.

'What is it about you, Chesnie Davenport?' he asked, and when, feeling slightly bemused, she couldn't give him an answer, went on, explaining, 'Half my time I expect you to jump one way—and you constantly surprise me by jumping the other.'

'What did I say?' she wanted to know, and felt him move. All at once he was lying on his side, resting on his forearm and looking down into her still delicately sleep-flushed face.

'How can you look so lovely?' he asked.

There was a tender light in her eyes, and as her pulses started to zip along so her brain started seizing up fast. 'Wh-what did I say?' she repeated, as she strove hard to pull herself together.

'This time?' He smiled gently. 'This time, almost in the same breath that you tell me you're a virgin, you...' his head started to come down '…invite me…' He paused, and his mouth was almost against hers when he breathed, 'To…' and said no more, but kissed her.

It was a wonderful kiss. Tender, yet seeking. A kiss like none they had shared before. Joel raised his head and looked into her eyes, as if expecting that she would raise some objection—but then hadn't he just stated that she never did what he expected half the time?

'That was—nice,' she said, and smiled.

'You and your invitations,' he grumbled, but was smiling too when he drew her close up to him.

'Oh, Joel,' she cried—a little shakily, it was true.

'Am I alarming you?'

She shook her head, and, wanting quite desperately that he should kiss her again, replied openly, 'I—er—wouldn't mind—er—knowing more, actually,' and was rewarded with a kiss that left her feeling quite breathless.

Then Joel was pulling back to look into her lovely green eyes—and, as if satisfied that she wasn't put off, that she still wanted to know more, 'You're so sweet,' he breathed, and the next moment she was being kissed in a way that made her realise she had never truly been kissed before. His tongue caressed her lips and her whole being seemed to tremble in his arms.

She loved him, and loved the sensations he was creating in her body. She had no power to push him away, and as she felt his hands caressing her spine, drawing her yet closer to him, she did not want to push him from her.

But even as he was kissing her suddenly it was Joel who was doing the pushing away. Unexpectedly, abruptly, he was suddenly wrenching his mouth from hers. 'No,' he groaned on a strangled kind of sound.

'No?' she echoed, utterly confused.

'We—have to stop.' The words seemed to be dragged from him.

'Stop?' Her wits had flown. But Joel was breaking from

her, moving swiftly to the side of the bed, grabbing up his trousers.

Chesnie was staring at him dumbfounded when, 'Here endeth the first lesson!' he ground out, and in one movement seemed to be in his trousers, and snaking on his shirt as he went, and was out through the door.

CHAPTER NINE

PRIDE was her only friend on that drive back to London. Chesnie knew full well from his terse silence that Joel was very much regretting having stepped through the platonic barrier—even if he did seem to think she had invited him over that particular threshold. To her chagrin, she could not say that she hadn't.

But by the time they arrived in London she had started to grow a little bit annoyed. Her sisters had the sort of marriages where they and their husbands went for days without speaking to each other. So, fine, the marriage she had with Joel was a vastly different affair—but, still the same, she had no intention of going down that same tortuous, less than monosyllabic road.

They were in the apartment and Joel was just about to go to his study when the steam valve on her temper blew. Though somehow she made herself sound calm as she called his name.

'Joel!' He turned, stony-expressioned, and her heart quailed—but she still wasn't having it. 'Apropos—er—sex and stuff—' she introduced the root evil of what this was all about '—I wonder if we can come to an agreement whereby if I promise to keep out of your bed, you promise not to show me lesson two?'

He didn't laugh, but his lips definitely twitched, she would swear. 'You're doing it again,' he said, and, at her look of enquiry, 'The unexpected. I was sure you'd want to avoid that subject like the plague!'

It was she who laughed, her temper gone, and they were friends again. Without another word she turned and, aware that he was watching her, breezed away and went to her room.

She did not see very much of him that day, but he came into her office the following day to discuss some business and to tell her that he was flying up to Glasgow that afternoon.

'I haven't any note of it in your diary,' she replied, her heart sinking; he had said nothing about her going with him.

'I'll probably be away a few days,' Joel replied, and went on to talk about other matters, and so obviously didn't care tuppence that he wouldn't see her for several days that Chesnie was sure that she didn't care either.

And, oh, what a liar pride had made of her. The evening stretched on and on endlessly without him. Even though she made a point of never being in the same room with him over-long, just to know he was under the same roof was a comfort to the love she had for him.

Chesnie had a vision of life without him in two years' time, and didn't like it. She gave herself a talking to. Subject: Don't get attached to him, you knew in advance that it wasn't going to last.

She finally went to bed, to lie awake determining that she was going to be more impersonal about this—she remembered his kisses, and for ageless minutes was lost in the wonder of the joy of those kisses. But, of course, those kisses were a 'one-off', never again to be repeated. So, yes, they had got personal, but they were both human and had said goodbye to a strictly business relationship on the day they had married.

But clearly Joel regretted those intimate moments they had shared, so from now on she would keep herself as aloof as possible away from the office. Which, since she had barely seen Joel since they had returned from Herefordshire, and was obviously the way Joel liked it, didn't look as though it would be any great problem.

Chesnie was still thinking 'aloof' when she drove to the

office the next day. Around eleven the phone rang, and as she recognised Joel's voice so 'aloof' started to slip.

'I—need you here,' he said. He didn't sound very inviting, but still the same her heart began to race. 'By the time you've briefed Eileen Gray to take over for you it will be too late to catch an earlier flight. You'd better take the one-fifteen from Heathrow,' he commanded. 'Today,' he added, and hung up. Chesnie made a face at the phone. Then she burst into smiles. So much for 'aloof'; she was going to see Joel!

She made Heathrow with little time to spare, and had just taken her seat aboard the aircraft when a late arrival came and took the seat next to her. He did a double-take and then beamed. 'Chesnie Cosgrove!'

'Philip!' She was surprised and pleased to see him, and smiled back.

'Had I known you were making the Glasgow trip I'd have sprinted twice as fast!' he exclaimed, then caught sight of her wedding band. 'Chesnie Davenport,' he corrected. 'I don't suppose you'd consider divorcing him?'

'I've only just married him! How's your new PA?'

'You'd have been better,' he said. 'Still working?'

'I'm on my way to assist Joel now.'

'Lucky devil!' Philip exclaimed, but went on, 'Of course. I've a meeting with Joel in the morning—I should have expected you'd be in Glasgow if he's there. You must know all about Yeatman's sniffing around after Symington Technology.'

She hadn't! Why hadn't Joel told her? She kept her composure to enquire lightly, 'How do you feel about it?' Didn't Joel trust her?

'My feelings are very mixed. Part of me says no; the other—'

'Philip, I'm sorry. I shouldn't have asked.' She stopped him right there. 'It was unfair of me.'

He turned his head and smiled at her. 'Because you're working for the other side?' She nodded, feeling guilty, but blaming her intrusion on the fact that, had she known in advance about Yeatman Trading 'sniffing around' with a view to taking over Symington Technology, she'd not have felt so shocked, and would have been more watchful of her tongue. Why would Joel keep something like that from her? 'You're lovely,' Philip said, and impulsively caught a hold of her hand. Bringing it to his mouth, he kissed the back of it. 'Your husband can't object to that,' he said, and Chesnie doubted that he would.

Throughout the rest of the journey she and Philip spoke of matters other than work, but Chesnie owned to feeling a touch hurt that Joel had not told her what, in her view—married to him or not—a confidential PA, a trusted PA, should know.

So much so that when Philip stated that, once his meeting was over that afternoon, it looked as though he was in for a solitary boring evening, she almost invited him to dine at her hotel. She was sorely tempted, she had to admit, and not entirely on account of Philip being alone and bored. She'd love to see Joel's face when he realised that as far as she was concerned he could keep his secrets—she knew about his proposed takeover anyway.

She did not invite Philip to dine with her because for one thing she was unsure, depending on how much work Joel had for her, if she would be having a 'working' dinner. For another, she didn't know if Joel would expect her to dine with him, and, since he had a meeting with Philip tomorrow, if to entertain him to dinner that night might pre-empt their business.

'Will you be at the meeting tomorrow?' Philip asked when, he going on to a different hotel, they shared a taxi from Glasgow airport.

'I'm not sure,' she replied. 'I'll be busy one way or another, I'm sure of that,' she added lightly.

Philip saluted her cheek with a kiss as they parted. 'Bye, Chesnie,' he bade her, and she almost wished it was him that she loved, but she didn't love him—and the man she did love didn't trust her.

She was expected at the hotel and went up in the lift to the same suite she and Joel had occupied before. While knowing that he would be either at his desk or round some conference table working, she still felt a little breathless in case Joel had already returned from his labours.

Illogical? Call it love. She sighed. She had the suite to herself for a while, by the look of it. Yet, even while she wasn't very sure that she felt too friendly towards Joel, she still the same went to the mirror, ran a comb through her hair and renewed her lipstick.

Chesnie glanced at her watch. There was still a large part of the afternoon left—hours before she could expect to see Joel. What was she supposed to do? He knew what time she was arriving. He'd been the one to tell her which flight to catch. Did he expect her to sit and twiddle her thumbs for the rest of the afternoon?

She half decided to take a taxi to the company offices, then thought that if Joel had wanted her to go to Yeatman House he'd have said so. Which meant he didn't need her there so urgently that she'd had to catch that lunchtime flight after all.

Why hadn't he told her that he was looking into a deal with Symington's? If he had a meeting with Philip tomorrow, then obviously negotiations were either under way or about to happen. Presumably Glasgow had been chosen for the negotiations to limit any possible hint to the press at this early stage.

Feeling hurt at her exclusion, Chesnie was half minded to leave the hotel and go and take a look at the shops. Then she realised that, since Joel seldom did anything without a purpose, he would probably telephone with some work instruction. He knew what time her flight got in.

Chesnie waited a half-hour. No call. A half-hour later, leaving the bathroom door ajar just in case, she went and had a bath. An hour after that she changed into an outfit which would suffice should she have dinner at her work table or in the hotel's dining room.

Joel arrived at a little after seven. Chesnie pinned a smile on her face. He did not smile—she wondered why she had bothered. 'Long day?' she asked sweetly.

'I've had longer,' he grunted, and, loosening his tie as he went, he made for his bedroom.

Chesnie disappeared into her room. If he wanted her he knew where she was. She heard him taking a shower, and her feeling of mutiny began to weaken. Poor love, he'd most likely slaved away all day. What he didn't need at the end of it was a sulky assistant.

She went into the sitting room. A short while later he joined her. 'Are we eating here, or downstairs?' she enquired pleasantly.

He looked at her, seemed to look at her long and hard, and then he smiled. 'Thank you for coming.'

She wanted to say something casual such as, It's my job, but she'd have flown to him without that. 'Anything for you,' she said, and offered him a cheeky grin so he'd know she didn't mean it.

'That impudent mouth of yours will get you into trouble one of these days,' he commented, his glance automatically finding her lips—but he seemed to have recovered his good humour.

Impudent mouth? How could he say that? She'd thought she was the very soul of discretion and sobriety. However, it appeared there were matters buzzing in Joel's head, so they worked for an hour, then had dinner sent up, and worked some more. But at no time did Joel mention what all the time she had been expecting, hoping, he would mention—the Symington Technology negotiations.

By the time they had finished their work for the evening Chesnie was having to work hard in another direction—to hide her feelings. 'Time for a little relaxation, I think,' Joel remarked. 'You can finish that lot tomorrow. I've an appointment at eight, so I'll be out of your way until some time in the late afternoon.'

'You want me to stay here in Glasgow?'

'You need to go back tomorrow?' he asked sharply.

He annoyed her. 'Not particularly,' she answered—and was faintly amazed to see Joel take what appeared to be a controlling breath.

'Can I get you a drink?' he asked evenly.

'No, thank you. I think I'll go to bed.'

She didn't look at him, but left him and went to her room. Then hated that she had to leave her room to go to the bathroom for her habitual shower before she got into bed.

He was seated on the sofa when she went through. She rather thought he seemed a shade fed-up about something, but she wasn't looking at him long enough to be certain. Not that she cared anyhow. She stood beneath the shower, not bothered a button that he might be fed-up.

That made two of them that were fed-up. So he'd had a bad day—her day hadn't been too brilliant either. From where she was viewing it, it didn't seem very nice at all to discover in a roundabout way—even if those talks were secret—that her boss didn't trust her enough to let her into that secret. That her husband didn't trust her enough—

Abruptly she broke off such thought. He wasn't her husband—except on paper. She… Chesnie blanked off more thoughts and stepped out of the shower. She dried herself and got into her nightdress and cotton wrap, still trying to keep weakening thoughts at bay.

'Goodnight!' she offered crisply as, with her bundle of clothes under one arm, she went quickly through the sitting room.

Joel stood up, as though he perhaps wanted to have a word with her, but she wasn't stopping to listen. He had not returned her goodnight when she went into her room and closed the door on him.

And that was when she thought, Dammit, I'm not having

this, and, dropping her bundle of clothes down on a chair, stormed back to the door and wrenched it open—and came face to face with Joel.

'I was just coming to see you,' he stated calmly.

'Snap!' she retorted hostilely.

He studied her angry expression. 'By the look of you, you'd better go first.'

She waited for no further invitation, but, having stewed for long enough over the issue, exploded, 'You have a meeting with Philip Pomeroy tomorrow!' and saw straight away from the look of fury on Joel's face at the mention of Philip's name that she was correct in her thinking that Joel did not want her to know anything about it.

'He told you that, did he?' Joel charged tersely.

'*You* didn't!' she answered angrily, and waited for him to tell her why he hadn't.

But to her amazement he declined to make any explanation whatsoever, and questioned instead, 'You flew up with him?'

What had that got to do with anything? 'Philip was on the same plane.'

'Cosy!' Joel snarled. Then, sharply, 'By prior arrangement?' he demanded.

'What?' Chesnie wasn't with him.

'You and Pomeroy—you've been in touch with him all along? You never—'

'Don't be…' She began to fire, then erupted in fury. 'You don't trust me!' she raged. 'If you did you'd have told me you were interested in Symington's, and not left me to find out from—'

'Pomeroy told you!'

'Why wouldn't he? *He* trusts me!'

'You're that close?' Joel snarled.

What the Dickens was he getting at? 'Close enough for me to consider inviting him here to dinner tonight!' she flew, refusing to back down.

'The devil you did!' Joel roared, his jaw jutting furiously.

'You're married *to me*, remember!' he barked, his hands coming to her upper arms, biting into her flesh.

But she still wasn't having it. 'Only for the next two years!' she retaliated, sparks flashing in her lovely green eyes.

'He'll wait?' Joel thundered. She shrugged, and let him think what he would. He apparently didn't like the answer his thoughts had brought him, for angrily he drew her hard up against him, his arms coming round her, and the next she knew Joel was punishing her mouth with a kiss of un-restrained fury.

And Chesnie hated it. And she fought him. She wanted his kisses, but not like this. But his grip on her was un-breakable, and that punishing kiss deepened until at last she managed to drag her mouth away from his. *'No!'* she cried on a half-sob, but for a while she was still fastened to him in his rock-hard hold.

Until suddenly, abruptly, he let her go, all tension and fury seeming to melt from him. 'I'm—sorry,' he apologised on a hoarse breath of sound. His face appearing to have lost some of its colour, he groaned, 'Oh, my dear, I've frightened you half to death,' and while Chesnie, her anger and fury gone too, stared into his remorse-filled expression, 'I don't want to hurt you,' Joel murmured.

And this—his remorse, *his* obvious hurt—she could not take. 'It's all right,' she whispered. 'Oh, Joel, it's all right.' And, her heart his, her love all his, she stretched up and gently kissed him. 'I'm not frightened,' she tried to gently assure him. And, smiling, hoping to elicit a smile from him, 'I just don't care much for being kissed like that.'

'My dear,' he said softly, and as she had gently kissed him so he gently kissed her. 'Is that better?'

Her heart was beating nineteen to the dozen. 'Much,' she answered softly, and somehow they were kissing again.

Tender, gentle kisses. Kisses that wiped away all anger and pain. Kisses that Chesnie never wanted to stop. She loved him, was in love with him, and just then could think of nothing but the joy of being in his arms.

'We should stop,' Joel breathed against her ear.

He had said something similar before—and she had felt bereft when he'd taken his arms away from her. 'Why?' she whispered.

'Why? Because... Because you're making it difficult for me to think clearly.'

She smiled. 'This is no time for thinking clearly,' she laughed.

'Oh, Chesnie,' he breathed helplessly, and gathered her more closely in his arms.

Quite when they had moved away from the door and further into her room Chesnie had no idea, but suddenly she became aware that they were nearer to her bed than to the door. She saw Joel follow her glance.

'This is where you say, "It's been nice knowing you, but..."' he teased softly.

And Chesnie kissed him. 'You know I seldom say what you expect me to say,' she answered dreamily, and as his brow lifted in surprised comprehension she didn't care that she had just given him full permission to kiss her again and again. She heard him groan, as if he were fighting a battle within himself. Then she felt the pressure of his arms about her increase. But, fearing that was a prelude to him removing his arms from her completely, she kissed him, and held him, and then to her joy felt him returning her kiss. And all at once, as he parted her lips with his own, he was arousing in her such a vortex of feeling that she could barely think.

Joel's kisses to her throat and shoulders thrilled her anew. She was vaguely aware that he was removing her cotton wrap, vaguely aware that she stood before him in nothing but her thin cotton nightdress, vaguely aware that he was shirt and trouser-clad, but nothing mattered as he gathered her to him, his hands caressing over her back, down to her hips, and caressing until his hand captured her pert behind, holding her, drawing her against him.

Willingly, if a little unsure, she pressed into him, her arms up and over his shoulders, and felt near to collapsing against him when his hands caressed over her body until tenderly he captured one breast in a gentle hold.

She supposed she must have made some small sound for he asked softly, albeit his warm hand stayed at her breast, 'Is this all right with you, Chesnie?'

She smiled up at him. 'It's—er—a bit wonderful,' she answered shyly, and asked, 'May I do the same to you?'

He laughed lightly; it was a lovely sound in her ears. 'Come here,' he said, and kissed her, caressed her, and, her nightdress a hindrance, he slipped it from her shoulders. Then he kissed her again before, pulling back, he bent his head to her naked breasts.

She swallowed hard, her insides a riot of emotion as he raised his head, and while caressing the hardened peaks of her breasts he kissed her.

Her nightdress fell to the floor. 'You're blushing,' he teased tenderly. What could she do? She raised her hands and began to unfasten his shirt, and he smiled, his eyes steady on hers until, as bare-chested as her breasts were, he drew her against him and she entered a world of pure delight.

More enchantment was hers when, unhurriedly, without haste, he moved with her to the bed. They kissed again, and again, and a fever of wanting started to mount in her. That fever wanted only one kind of release when she found she was lying with Joel, their legs mingling, and realisation came to her that he was no longer wearing trousers.

He gently moved her until she was lying with her back against the mattress. Then, lying on his side but keeping some daylight between their two bodies, Joel looked deeply into her eyes. 'Help me here, Chesnie,' he requested.

'How?' she asked huskily, feeling too bemused just then to be able to decipher what he meant.

'I want, quite desperately, to make love to you—but I'm unsure…'

'Oh, Joel.' Her heart was leaping about like nobody's business. 'I—I think I want to make love with you too.'

'Think?' he queried, and, when she was desperate to feel him close again, not coming any nearer.

She gave him a tremulous smile, then told him honestly, 'I think I'm a bit nervous about—about—close intimacy, but I've never felt like this before, and I don't think I could bear it if you left me without—' She broke off, that shyness she had spoken of causing her to be unable to finish.

But Joel seemed to know, and to understand, and suddenly she had her wish and he came closer and began creating such a fire in her she could barely breathe from the emotion of it. She felt his hands caressing over her back, staying there, allowing her to get used to his touch, to feel comfortable with his touch. Then, causing that fire in her to blast off anew, his hands caressed down to the delicious naked curves of her behind. She moaned a sigh of bliss, of wanting, and he seemed to understand, and came closer to her, his body half over hers. And she wanted to feel more of him, and her hands instinctively found the back of the only item of clothing he wore. She thrilled anew as she placed her hands inside and, with fingers caressing his well-shaped buttocks, pulled him to her.

There was no going back then. She knew it as he rolled from her to remove that article of clothing and then feast his eyes on her body, to stroke and to caress, to take her breasts in turn into his mouth, while at the same time, in gradual sensitive seeking, one hand caressed tenderly down over her body to make her gasp in shyness and rapture.

'Oh, Joel!' she cried, her voice all kind of wobbly.

But he seemed to know of both her shyness and her need, and what her cry had been all about, for he kissed her, rousing her to arch herself to him and, his touch becoming yet more intimate, causing her to gasp. Joel took time for her to make that big adjustment to such private intimacy and, as a sigh whispered from her, 'Soon, my love,' he murmured. 'Soon.'

Chesnie slept but briefly after she and Joel, because of her untried body, had made slow-tempered, wonderful love. 'Sleep now,' he'd said softly, and to her delight had made no move to go to his own bed but, as naked as she, their passion spent, had tenderly kissed her, holding her against him. She had gone to sleep in his arms.

She was still in his arms about an hour later, but had moved to be lying on her side, with Joel's body fitting to the curve of hers. His hand was on her naked belly, and she wanted to turn and kiss him, marvelling at the tenderness he had shown her, the unsuspected gentleness of this man whom she knew could be quite hard in some of the tough business decisions he was called upon to make.

She did not turn to kiss him but lay still, her heart full as she recalled the tenderness of his touch, his gentleness and understanding, his utter unselfishness when she'd experienced a few difficulties at the outset. He had instantly stilled, and had oh, so tenderly kissed her. 'There's no hurry, my darling, no hurry at all,' he had breathed, and kissed her again. And she had wanted him so much, and had so much wanted to give him pleasure that she had moved first—to offer him her body—with love. And Joel had tenderly, and as slowly as her virginal body would allow, accepted.

Chesnie fell asleep again, thinking of the wonder of his lovemaking, thinking of that heady closeness they had shared. The next time she awakened—Joel had gone!

Instantly she missed him—and wanted him back with her. Why hadn't he wakened her? Why had he left—just like that, without a word? While she found it fairly incredible that Joel should have removed himself from the bed they had been sharing without her waking, she found it even more incredible that she—a light sleeper, for goodness' sake—had overslept that morning!

Her cheeks flushed with pink when the answer to tha
hit her full square—she and Joel had been making slow
unhurried love well into the night. Was it any wonder she
had slept soundly? The only wonder was that Joel had been
able to surface so early.

But then, he was probably used to this sort of thing
Suddenly, abruptly, that was when, in the cold light of day
thoughts began to surface which she did not want to surface. And she hurriedly got out of bed and headed for the
shower before spiteful darts of jealousy could throw more
unwanted spears.

Under the shower she tried her hardest to think logically
Joel had a meeting at eight, for goodness' sake! For all she
knew his meeting could be on the other side of the city
Given that most cities had a traffic problem at that hour in
the morning, was it likely, since he was probably hosting
that meeting, that he would hang around the hotel until five
minutes before the meeting was due to start? He had probably left just after seven...

Chesnie got out of the shower, dried and dressed, and
was still trying to think logically when she went into the
sitting room. She tried hard to convince herself that it was
out of consideration for her that Joel hadn't wakened her—
then found that she was looking for a note, looking for
some sign that it hadn't been purely just sex for him.

There was no note—and that was when she came to with
a bump. What else did she think it was other than purely
sex, for heaven's sake? So, yes, Joel had used a few en-
dearments, a few encouraging kisses when she'd had a few
initial problems, but the words had meant nothing to him
Oh, what a fool she would be to dwell on that encouraging
'my darling'—or any of it, for that matter.

She didn't want breakfast and sat down at her work table
striving hard for some kind of professionalism to cope with
the work she had to do.

But in her endeavours to pin her thoughts on something
else she failed miserably. She wanted Joel to love her, and

he didn't. She wanted him to have made love to her with love for her in his heart—fate cackled with mirth at such a ridiculous notion. Chesnie had to face the truth—that Joel's lovemaking had started from his fury with her, and that, quite plainly, all their lovemaking had meant to him was a release from his anger.

She forced herself to make a start on some work, but at nine o'clock she knew it was decision-time. She could not work. To sit there and to try and concentrate on complicated matter which yesterday she had been able to decipher with ease, today seemed totally beyond her. In fact, the way she felt then, Chesnie was of the opinion she would never have that capability again.

And it was Joel's fault. He had last night lifted her up to the heights, and this morning—she had come crashing down. She wished that she could hate him for it, but she could not. Because, basically, it was *not* his fault but hers. She, after all, in all of her actions, had given him the go-ahead all the way. Oh, the shame of it! Chesnie leapt up from her chair, her thoughts unsustainable. She knew then, without having to think about it, what she must do.

It was time to get out. Time to leave Joel, and her job with him. It was her only option; she saw that now if she could see nothing else. To stay, to carry on working for him, to go away with him again, to risk some point of disagreement cropping up—heaven knew what—she was too panic-stricken to know—and the same thing could happen if Joel kissed her again. She would be lost; she knew that she would.

A half-hour later and she was on her way to the airport. She had resigned. She did not have to put her resignation into writing. Joel would know that she did not intend to work for him again when he returned to the hotel—late that afternoon, he'd said—and discovered she had walked out on the job. Left without completing the work in hand. Not that the work was work which Eileen Gray could not take over, anyhow. From what Chesnie could make out it was not all that confidential. It was nothing to do with Symington Technology anyway.

Chesnie caught the ten-thirty flight and landed in London at midday. Her thoughts during that flight were tortuous. She drove to the home she shared with Joel plagued by doubts now that she had thought of Symington Technology—Joel had only made love to her on account of his fury that she might be 'playing around' with Philip Pomeroy. Joel's fury that, while married to him, she might be intending perhaps to break their 'no indulgence with the opposite sex while married' agreement. Joel was a man of his word; he wouldn't think very much of her breaking hers.

Chesnie sighed as she let herself into their home. Joel wouldn't want her under his roof now. She had better go and pack her belongings. It would be less painful if she did it now, while Joel was out of the way in Scotland.

She supposed if Joel were returning to London that night he would catch either the six-thirty or the seven-thirty flight. Whatever time he arrived home, though, she was sure he would certainly not expect to find her there when he got in.

Just the same, Chesnie found she had a need to take a final look around his home before she went to pack. She wandered from room to room, trying to clear her head of the memory of Joel's tenderness with her last night. But in remembering his tenderness she began to grow confused. Recalling Joel's considerate lovemaking, she began to wonder had he really made love to her on account of her 're-lationship' with Philip? Joel's lovemaking had been sweet and gentle, not harsh and vengeful.

But—what did she know? Chesnie cogitated that, inexperienced as she had been, would she have known the difference? With demons of doubt chasing her, she went and got out her cases.

She was halfway through her packing, and was hurting so much she could barely think straight, when she began to realise that, should Joel come home tonight, then tonight or possibly first thing tomorrow morning she was going to have to have some sort of conversation with him. She'd have to do that by telephone. She wasn't ready to speak with Joel face to face yet—she had no idea if she ever would be. But when she was back in her old flat, when she felt calmer, she would ring him and explain that she had realised she didn't want to stay living with him—oh, what a lie that was—and that while he was at liberty to make up whatever he wished to explain her leaving Yeatman Trading she was perfectly willing, in the interests of him securing the chairmanship, to attend any function with him that he deemed necessary.

Having reached that conclusion, Chesnie felt very much like bursting into tears, and heartily wished she had never flown up to Glasgow yesterday. Though, if she had not, if that situation had never got out of hand, she would never have known the exquisite joy of Joel's lovemaking.

Cackling fate must be having a wonderful time at her expense, she mused unhappily. She had never wanted marriage. A year ago, six months ago, even three months ago, she would have run like blazes in the opposite direction. Now here she was married—well and truly married, thanks to last night—and when she and Joel had always been going to be divorced anyway, here she was—wanting to stay married.

She bit her lip to stop herself from crying—then heard a sound that made her spin round. A gasp of shock left her, and scarlet colour rioted through her skin.

She had thought she was not yet ready to speak face to face with Joel—but it didn't look as if she had very much choice in the matter. So taken up with her thoughts had she been, she had not heard him come in!

'H-how...?' she stammered, then grabbed at a passing snatch of her former calm. 'What time did you get in?' she asked, her racing heartbeats thundering in her ears.

Joel looked steadily back at her, not a smile about his

features. 'At a guess I'd say my plane touched down forty-five minutes after yours,' he answered evenly. Then, his glance going from her scarlet face to her almost full suitcase, his expression grew tough. 'What, would you mind telling me, do you think you're doing?' he demanded curtly.

CHAPTER TEN

WHAT did she think she was doing? She'd have thought that was fairly obvious. 'I—thought I'd leave—if that's all right with you,' Chesnie answered, never knowing from where she found such a cool, controlled tone.

She saw a muscle jerk in his temple. 'Actually, it isn't all right with me,' he responded, and sounded as tough as he looked. 'It's very far from all right with me!'

'I'm s-sorry you feel that way,' Chesnie replied, her controlled tone starting to fracture. 'Naturally I'll attend any function with you that you'd—'

'All this because we made love?' Joel cut her off harshly, causing colour to rush to her face again. Scarlet which Joel observed. 'Oh, Chesnie,' he said, his tough tone at once evaporating. 'Was it so very dreadful for you that—?'

'No!' She stopped him abruptly. Their lovemaking had been beautiful; she had been enraptured by his tenderness and sensitivity. Whatever else he believed she just could not let him believe it had been dreadful for her. But, not wanting him to read any kind of emotion in her face, she turned her back on him. 'It wasn't dreadful at all,' she denied huskily.

She heard him move and knew he was right behind her when he said close by, 'If it's not that, then something else has upset you. Something equally major—you are meaning to leave me *and* your job, aren't you?'

Dumbly, she nodded, and felt more churned up than ever inside when Joel gently took a hold of her shoulders and turned her to face him. She didn't want to look at him, but after long seconds of silence she couldn't bear it and raised

167

her head, and found herself looking into a pair of extremely serious steady blue eyes.

Hot colour flared in her face again as, while looking into his eyes, she recalled their lovemaking, that ultimate intimacy they had shared. But as she looked at him so Joel looked back at her, and observed the waves of colour ebbing and flowing to her face. 'Poor love, you're in one almighty emotional whirlpool, aren't you?' he said softly.

'I'm n—' She would have attempted to deny it.

'And that's entirely understandable.' Joel gently cut through her denial. 'You have shared with me a most precious and special time,' he stated with a smile, 'and it's rather shaken you.' His smile faded. 'But, since I'm obviously the root cause of why you want to go, and that special time is obviously the trigger, don't you think that maybe we should talk about it first?'

Chesnie looked at him in alarm. 'That's the last thing I want to talk about!' she retorted swiftly—he was being too understanding; it was unnerving. 'I j-just want to pack my cases and be gone.'

'And to blazes with what I want?'

'I've already said I'm willing to attend any functions with you in regard to you getting the chairmanship!' she retaliated.

And was left staring at him dumbstruck when, as clear as anything, so she knew she hadn't misheard him, he retorted, 'To hell with the chairmanship—I'm talking about you and me!' Chesnie was still staring at him open-mouthed when he caught hold of her arm. 'We need to talk this through, Chesnie. We'll go into the drawing room.'

She didn't want to talk at all, and could only think that she must still be stunned by his declared 'To hell with the chairmanship', because she allowed him to guide her from the bedroom to the drawing room. To be chairman was what he had wanted above all else.

Chesnie realised she was still not functioning properly in that she discovered she was seated on one end of the sofa,

Joel at the other, without quite knowing how she had got there.

But this would never do. She sought and found some backbone and turned in her seat to look at Joel—he was already turned facing her, she discovered, and went all weak inside again. How dear he was, how tender his caresses... 'It's better this way!' she gabbled in a rush.

'Why?' Joel asked, and she supposed she should have seen that coming. She had worked for him long enough to know that, if it interested him, what he didn't know he always dug at until he found out. She had no answer. None that she was prepared to give him anyway. 'I'm assuming here,' he went on, when he obviously thought he had waited long enough, 'that your decision to go has nothing to do with Philip Pomeroy.'

'Philip Pomeroy!' she exclaimed, her look of amazement that Joel could think such a thing enough of a denial.

'And, since you've intimated you didn't find our love-making offensive—'

'I honestly don't want to talk about this,' Chesnie interrupted him, going pink again.

Joel smiled gently, but was determined, nevertheless, and reminded her, 'We had an understanding, you and I, that you would stay married to me for two years. That you would live with me for two years—'

'We can still stay married,' she butted in. 'I have no problem with that,' she added hurriedly—and could have groaned out loud.

As she had immediately realised, Joel wasn't likely to miss the implication of that last hastily added bit. 'But you have a problem living with me?' he questioned.

'I...' she answered helplessly. Then made desperate attempts to get herself more of one piece. 'I'm going,' she said, but her attempt to get to her feet didn't get very far. She had moved fast, but Joel had moved faster, and before she knew it she was again sitting on the sofa, only this time she was blocked in by the sofa arm on one side and Joel on the other.

She admitted she felt shaken, but she was even more shaken when Joel, an angry Joel, suddenly rounded on her, accusing harshly, 'You walk in, disrupt my life, and then, entirely without explanation, calmly think you can walk out again?' He shook his head. 'It's not on, Chesnie.'

She stared at him, opening her mouth to protest—disrupt his life!—then gained her second wind. 'What about me?' she challenged. *Calmly* think? She couldn't just then remember the last time she had thought calmly when she thought of Joel.

'What about you?' Joel asked, not letting up on the determined stance he was taking. 'Tell me about you. Tell me what this is all about,' he demanded.

She didn't want to answer, but saw no let-up in his determined manner. 'I don't want meaningless sex!' she blurted out, at once wished she hadn't, and strove hard to discover if she had revealed too much.

'Who—?' Joel broke off. He had appeared ready to argue but seemed to swiftly change his mind—as though, having got her to start talking, he wanted to hear more. 'Go on,' he encouraged.

She didn't want to go on, but she was still wedged in, she could feel his thigh warm up against her thigh—it didn't help very much. 'I…' She hesitated, but by his very silence he was making her go on. 'If I st-stay working for you, then at some time or other I'll have to go away with you again. I—don't know what happens. That is to say, I'm unsure what— Anyhow, if we erupt into an argument again—if you kiss me again—' She broke off helplessly, wishing so much that she had never got started—but still Joel's very silence was goading her on. 'Well…' she was floundering '…you know what could happen.'

'It could just as well happen here,' he pointed out quietly, his eyes on her face, studying, assessing.

'No,' Chesnie denied. 'It wouldn't. Here you allow me

my own space. Your ethics wouldn't allow you to violate that—'

'You feel I *violated* you?' Joel broke in, looking and sounding absolutely appalled.

'*No!*' she denied, outraged at the very thought. 'Of course I don't! What we... Our... You were wonderful with me,' she admitted, her face on fire again, but loving him too much to ever let him hate himself for those moments they had shared. 'You were so patient, so understanding. You made that time beautiful for me,' she said. But, knowing she was crimson, she began to fear that in her earnestness to assure him she didn't feel in the least violated, she might have said too much. 'I'd better go,' she decided urgently.

'No!' Joel denied her, putting out a hand to restrain her. His touch unnerved her. 'You'll get the chairmanship without any—'

'Did you not hear me? I'm not bothered about the chairmanship.'

'Yes, you are!' she argued. 'You're ambitious and—'

'Let me qualify that,' Joel cut in, then strangely he paused and seemed to take a deep breath. 'Chesnie Davenport,' he resumed, looking nowhere but into her lovely green eyes, 'I have lately come to realise that if you are not in my life, then nothing else matters.' And, when Chesnie, her eyes huge, just stared at him dumbstruck, 'I don't give a damn about being chairman if you're not there with me,' he ended.

'B-but it *is* your life!' she stammered—and was left dizzy with emotion at his answer.

'Chesnie, *you're* my life,' he told her. She swallowed hard and just continued to stare at him, wide-eyed. 'Everything I've achieved or want in life is worthless if you're not there to share it with me,' he went on, taking her breath away and causing her to be for the moment incapable of speech. 'And as for making love with you being meaningless, you couldn't have it more wrong.'

'I—c-couldn't?' Was that husky squeak of a voice hers? Her heart was beating so fast she felt she would faint. Happiness, incredible joy, was pushing to break through, caution holding it back.

'You have high values, Chesnie, and I like that. But don't sell me short.'

'I—um…'

'My dear,' Joel murmured, 'don't you know your sweet response to me last night made my heart rejoice? I couldn't believe we were going to make love, that you…'

'I didn't want you to stop,' she whispered involuntarily.

'Oh, sweet darling,' Joel breathed, and, as if he truly had to know, 'Tell me you care for me a little,' he urged. 'Tell me you'll stay.'

Chesnie was such a bundle of nerves by then, still uncertain for all she had never seen him look so sincere, that nothing would get that sort of confession from her. 'Which one would you like to hear first?' she prevaricated.

'The one follows the other.' He looked into her eyes, and waited. Then, placing an arm about her shoulders, he lightly kissed the corner of her mouth. 'You're not going to tell me, are you?' he questioned. She would not answer. But, since she wasn't attempting to leap up again and leave, he seemed to grow a fraction less tense than he had been, and took time to explain, 'I didn't want to leave at all this morning. You looked so adorable lying there.'

'You didn't—wake me.'

'I was afraid to,' he confessed softly. 'I wanted to kiss you awake, but had to go quickly. I feared, had I kissed you, you might be as welcoming as you had been a few hours earlier. Then—' He broke off as a tide of pink crept under her skin.

He seemed unable to resist the allure of her lips, and bent his head and kissed her—and at the feel of his lips on hers everything in Chesnie started to go haywire. She pushed at his chest. He broke his kiss and pulled back, his expression grave.

'I've read the situation wrong!' he exclaimed shakenly.

'I need to think,' Chesnie replied. 'And—and you're making thinking very difficult.'

A slow smile started to spread across his features. 'Because I kissed you, dare I hope?'

'I don't know what it is—I've never been like this.'

'I understand,' he said softly.

'I've been kissed before, b-but I've never gone so wildly out of control before.'

'I know,' he repeated with a tender smile. He looked as though he might kiss her again, but suggested, 'If I've worked this out correctly—and what you've just said seems to confirm it—you, my darling, are just a little bit in love with me.'

Chesnie jerked away from him, but was still held firmly in the curve of his arm. She was just a very great deal in love with him, she would have said, but was feeling so jumpy inside that there was no way she was going to admit it. 'How did you come to that conclusion?' she enquired, while wondering if she was being wise or foolish. She had countless times seen him work through the most complicated of issues, casting aside irrelevant parts until he came up with the answer—was she leaving herself totally without cover? But, to a certain extent, she had that methodical ability too, and all at once her confused thoughts were clearing and she was doing some analysing of her own. Taking into account what she knew of him, she was then adding it to the memory of having lain in his sensitive and caring embrace—and all of a sudden she was starting to believe the unbelievable; that perhaps, just perhaps, Joel's caring might extend beyond the warm glow of their intimacy together. She jerked a look at him—but still wasn't ready to tell him what he wanted to know.

As if he understood, he smiled down at her and answered her question first. 'I've had a plane journey of one and a quarter hours in which to concentrate my thoughts solely on why, when we had been so at one with each other, you would take flight—not only leaving me, but, when your pride in your work is second to none, feeling you had to decamp leaving your work unfinished. Not to say barely touched. You weren't angry with me like the time before, when you went home—the reverse, in fact.'

'I—er… You weren't expecting to return to the hotel until late this afternoon,' Chesnie reminded him quickly.

'How could I concentrate on a meeting when thoughts of you were filling my head?' he asked.

'Really?' she questioned in wonder.

'Really,' Joel confirmed. 'Throughout that first tedious meeting with Pomeroy all I could think of was you, how you had been, how you had looked as I left, with your hair all loose and soft about your lovely head. I wanted to be back with you. That meeting finished at ten, for Pomeroy to go into discussions with his team and me to mine. I decided to delegate—we have a first-class team in Glasgow, as you know. I dashed back to the hotel—only to be informed, when I couldn't find a trace of you, that you'd taken a taxi to the airport. I couldn't believe it!'

'Oh, Joel,' she mourned, guilt swamping her. He did care for her! He must!

'You can be quite wicked when you put your mind to it,' he accused, but didn't seem to hold it against her. For he favoured her with a heart-melting tender look and told her, 'I hared after you, knowing in advance I wasn't going to make the same flight anyway.'

'You caught the next plane?'

'And,' he took up carefully, 'had time on the flight to recall again how lovely you had been—how shy, how innocent, but how wholly giving you had been with me. Giving as you had been with no man. And then all at once, my darling, my heart started to pound away as I thought about you, thought of the self-contained person you normally are, and I suddenly started to realise that there was no way, *absolutely no way*, you would have made love with me—unless you loved me a little.'

'You're—um—too clever by half,' Chesnie mumbled, feelings of joy refusing to be denied and starting to push through. As Joel seemed to have learned a lot about her, she too, she realised, had learned a lot about him. By the same token it seemed to her, then, that there was no way Joel would have told her of his findings—no way, since he did not want her to leave, he would have told her any of this—if he…did not love her a little in return!

'I don't know about clever,' he answered. 'Just tell me, am I accurate? Do you have any love for me?'

He was tense again, she noted, that arm about her taut as he waited. She gave in—partially. 'I suppose you could say that I—um—care as much for you as you appear to care for me.' She shyly understated the depth of her love for him, and saw that muscle jerk a beat in his temple again.

'You're saying, then, that I'm in your head night and day? That you can't eat or sleep for thinking of me? That you get up in the morning with me in your head, are restless and have taken to prowling about your bedroom, have known wild, unreasoning jealousy—and yet have stubbornly been refusing to acknowledge what is wrong with you?'

'You—care for me like that?' Chesnie asked on a whisper of sound.

'I love you like that—and more,' Joel corrected, and, while her heart raced, drew her into both his arms and gently kissed her. When he pulled back it was to look long and lingeringly into her face, and to ask, 'Would the extent of your caring begin with the letter "L"?'

Chesnie smiled. She loved him, and while it seemed incredible that he should return her love, she knew that as she trusted him, so she could trust his word. 'My caring for you begins with a very large capital "L",' she replied shyly.

'You love me?' It amazed her that he seemed to need to have it confirmed.

'Do you think I married you just to be the new chairman's PA?'

He was watching her, his clever intelligence reading every blink, every nuance. 'Why *did* you marry me, Chesnie?' he asked quietly.

She kissed him. 'Because I fell in love with you,' she answered simply—and was held, crushed up against his heart.

'Oh, Chesnie,' he breathed against her ear, and drew back to look into her face. 'You've loved me all these weeks? I can't believe it.' He kissed her, held her, and tenderly kissed her again. 'I need to know more,' he breathed. 'When, exactly?' he urged, and she laughed lightly. But as his tension left him, so her tension seemed to leave her.

'I didn't want to fall in love with you,' she felt she should tell him.

Then found he had worked that out for himself when he too gave a laugh, a loving laugh, and answered, 'Knowing you, I'm sure you kicked against it like the very devil.'

She kissed him, wanted to stay with him like this for ever, but sharing confidences like this was so wonderful she wanted to know more, to know absolutely everything. 'Was it like that for you too—refusing to acknowledge what those feelings were that got to me so many times?'

'The feeling of being irked—irrationally so?' he countered, and placed a light kiss on her mouth. 'You were so different from any other woman I've ever known,' he explained.

That surprised her. 'How?' She just had to know.

Joel settled her more comfortably in his arms. 'For a start, while a few other women I've known have declared they weren't interested in marriage, you were the only one I knew I could believe honestly and truthfully meant it.'

'That made you feel comfortable about it when you decided that to marry would give your chairmanship chances a boost?'

'You've been reading my mind.' He grinned. 'But it's for certain that when the idea came to me the notion to marry didn't panic me the way it would have done at one time—though only if you were my bride.' He paused, then with a self-deprecating smile added, 'The writing must have been on the wall then, only I failed to see it.'

'You decided to risk it?'

'What risk? I thought it all through. You had positively no wish to stay married and would be as keen as I to divorce in a couple of years' time, no harm done, no complications.' He looked into her eyes, his eyes alight with love as he went on, 'Only complications arose when I realised I was in love with you.'

'That upset your plans?'

'Made mincemeat of them,' he admitted, but didn't look too unhappy about it. 'Though I have to confess I had a regard for you that I'd never had for any other PA almost from the beginning.'

'Honestly?' she asked.

'I didn't own up to it—just wasn't ready to face what was happening to me,' he said with a smile that made her backbone melt. 'So why, when in the past I've had female staff who irritated me by batting their eyelashes at me every time I passed, did I feel a touch put out that my present PA was quite totally immune?' Chesnie smiled in love and wonder. 'It was only as it should be,' Joel continued, 'so why did I find that I wouldn't feel at all irritated, in fact wouldn't mind in the least should I spot a spark of interest from you in me.'

'Don't stop. I'm loving this,' Chesnie begged, her confidence in his love for her growing with every word he said.

He did stop, but only to place a loving kiss on her mouth. 'Then,' he resumed, 'in no time I'm seeing, and getting to know, a vastly different person from the cool and controlled woman I saw at interview.'

'You—um—saw through my cover?'

'I sussed that out quite quickly,' he agreed. 'At our first

meeting you were cool, sophisticated, elegant. Inside weeks of working with you I was discovering a woman who is sensitive and kind to the most junior members of staff— your kindness not confined to the post boy, but extended to my father. The goodness in you that you went to see him in your lunch-hour because you were worried about him...' Joel paused, and then confessed, 'I think love really started to hit me hard on our wedding day, when I saw another side of you—your gentle manner with your grandfather, your loyalty to your squabbling family. But,' he went on, giving her a look of mock severity, 'I kissed you—and all you could think about was your wretched gloves. Mrs Davenport, I am just not used to such treatment.'

'It—er—didn't seem appropriate to tell you that my knees were about to give way,' she answered, by way of apology.

Joel burst out laughing. 'Oh, you darling, you love!' he exclaimed, and just had to kiss her.

'They're giving way again!' she gasped, when he finally drew back.

'Oh, Chesnie Davenport,' he murmured. 'I'm trying with all I have to keep my head here, to content myself to enjoy these first precious moments of heart's-ease since last Saturday, when you put me in trauma by calmly getting into bed with me. And, as calmly and as cool as you please, asking me if I snore.'

'Cool! Calm!' She shook her head to disclaim any such suggestion, and then quickly picked up on what else he had just said. 'Trauma? You were in trauma?'

'I don't know what else you'd call it,' he replied, smiling tenderly at her. 'I was determined to keep to my side of the bed. No way, I told myself, did I want the complication of a consummated marriage. Then somehow during the night I felt you near—and for a brief while a wonderful tranquillity crept over me. I carefully gathered you in my arms and for the first time ever knew enchantment. I couldn't believe I should get such pleasure from just holding you quiet against me like that.'

Chesnie sighed blissfully. 'You knew—when I woke up, you knew I was awake?'

'I knew,' he replied, and kissed her hair as he had done then. 'I wanted us to stay like that, but...'

'But then I started issuing what you saw as an invitation,' she teased.

'Well, I wanted to kiss you anyway,' he laughed, and kissed her. But he pulled back to continue, 'Then my head started to have one gigantic battle with what I wanted to do, against what I should do. What was best for you, best for me...'

'You—um—got out of bed in a hurry.'

'Impudent madam,' he said lovingly. 'What else could I do? One of us had to be sensible— And you can blush.' He broke off to tease her, reminding her that she hadn't looked likely to be the one to put a stop to their lovemaking. 'I confess I wasn't thinking too clearly just then. But with what woolly-thinking capability I had, it seemed to me that if I took your innocence, as I wanted to, I would be causing us a whole heap of problems. Not least that I would have deemed our marriage permanent.'

'Oh,' she said, trying to keep up.

'Indeed,' he commented with a smile. 'So, as you rightly said, I got out of bed in a hurry—and that day went on to be the worst day of my life. I wanted to see you, needed to see you—and for my trouble felt I was going crazy because of you.'

'Joel!' she gasped on a whisper of breath.

'I was going to pieces over you,' he admitted. 'And on Monday, at the office, I found that to try and concentrate with your own good self in the next office was an impossibility. It was a great relief when all the preliminary skirmishing with Symington's culminated in a series of meetings being arranged at short notice. I was glad to be able to get away.'

'You—wanted to get away—from me?'

'I needed to think, my darling,' Joel explained tenderly. 'How could I think with you so near?'

'You needed to think about…?'

'About us. About you and me. I knew by then that I was head over heels in love with you. But what about you?'

'You had no idea?'

He shook his head. 'Not then. I couldn't even begin to reach any conclusion then. All I knew that Monday night in Glasgow was that I was there and you were in London—when what I wanted was that you should be with me. My love for you, sweet, beautiful Chesnie, was driving me crazy. I desperately needed to talk to you—to gauge, to try and work out if you loved me. So I decided that when I returned to London I'd casually suggest we have dinner somewhere, and I would fish to see how you felt. But that was when I realised—never having forgotten your nerve in turning down my first dinner invitation that day you lunched with my father—that you were just as likely to turn down my next one. I was in a complete stew about you, Chesnie,' he told her, to her delight and surprise. 'So on to plan B. If I could get you up to Glasgow…'

'It wasn't strictly necessary for me to go to Glasgow?' Chesnie exclaimed.

'I'm a swine,' he happily accepted. 'But, in my defence, I was suffering. Trust me, my darling, I wasn't thinking in terms of our sleeping together when I rang to ask you to catch that flight. All that was in my mind was that I couldn't bear being apart from you any longer and that once you were in Glasgow then, since we both had to eat, you could hardly turn down my dinner invitation. That would be when, rather than jump straight in and make a complete fool of myself, I might be able to test the water first. That was the plan—only by the time I saw you it had all started to get away from me.'

Never had she expected to hear that Joel had felt so vulnerable. 'Oh, my darling Joel,' she whispered softly, and warmly, tenderly, she kissed him.

'Chesnie.' He breathed her name, and close up to her informed her, 'I'm still trying desperately hard to keep my head here.'

She laughed—a light, never more happy laugh. 'Forgive me,' she apologised naughtily, and urged, 'And so?'

It took Joel a moment or two to recall where they had been. Then he was telling her, 'And so there was I, having given in to the desperate urge to see you, having formed my plan, having sent a car to the airport for you—which, incidentally, got stuck in traffic—but finding I'm unable to wait to see you. So unable to wait, in fact, that I ducked out of a meeting and grabbed a taxi at about the time I calculated you might have arrived at the hotel.'

'Your calculations were out by a good few hours,' she reminded him, recalling it had been early evening when he had returned to the hotel.

He shook his head, his handsome mouth picking up at the corners. 'They weren't,' he denied. 'I was in the taxi that pulled up behind yours. I saw Pomeroy kiss you—and managed to hang on to my sanity long enough to tell my driver to get us out of there.'

'You were at the hotel when...!' she exclaimed on a gasp, wonder taking her anew when it suddenly hit her that it wasn't so much the confidentiality of her work that made Joel dislike her going out with Philip, but... 'You were jealous!' she accused, barely believing what her intelligence had belatedly brought her. 'You were jealous of Philip!'

'I was as surprised as you—when I eventually owned up to the truth,' Joel admitted, and went on to explain, 'It was because I didn't want you having anything to do with Pomeroy that I didn't tell you we were putting out feelers for Symington's. Which,' he went on with a wry grin, 'makes rather a nonsense of me trying to convince myself, ever since he rang you at the office, that my dislike of you dating him was only because he was the opposition.'

'But it wasn't?' she pressed in delight.

'How could it be? I didn't care at all for the idea of him proposing to you. And in fact couldn't purchase an engagement ring fast enough so you might wear it on the night you told him we were to be married.'

'I didn't wear it that night,' Chesnie felt obliged to own.

'I realised, when I thought of your fine sensitivity, that you probably wouldn't,' he answered with a smile. 'I should have faced up to the fact that there was a great green-eyed monster sitting on my shoulder when it wasn't only Pomeroy I objected to asking you out but any other male who came into your office to ask you for a date.'

'Fergus Ingles?'

'The lot of them—him included.'

'Oh, Joel,' Chesnie sighed, and felt honour-bound to confess, 'I was not a little green-eyed myself, over Arlene Enderby.'

'Truly?' Joel enquired, seeming surprised.

'Truly,' Chesnie confirmed, and Joel borrowed some of her delight.

'I should have seen what was happening to me when, with thoughts of you somehow starting to occupy a lot of space in my head, I found I became quite evasive if any of my female acquaintances rang me. I should have realised I was in trouble way back, when you told me you'd no intention of becoming my stepmother! I discovered I didn't want you to be anybody's stepmother—in fact I didn't want you marrying anyone.'

Chesnie looked back at him wide-eyed. Then she laughed, a joy-filled laugh. 'You told yourself it was because, married, I—'

'Might give up your job and I would lose a terrific PA,' he finished for her. But his expression suddenly became so serious that Chesnie's own expression sobered. Her heart, which had been racing, leaping and generally beating out

all sorts of rhythms since she had turned round to see him
there with her in her bedroom, and not in Scotland, where
he should be, suddenly gave a lurch of dread.

'What? What's wrong?' she asked urgently.

'I hope nothing,' Joel replied. 'With all my heart I'm
hoping nothing's wrong. The reason I've taken time to explain a few things about how it is with me, the depth of
my love for you, my darling, is so you'll know and trust
that I will never harm you. And I hope that you'll...' he
paused, as if searching for just the right words '...that
you'll agree to a few changes in our lifestyle.'

She wasn't sure what he was asking, but to hear him say
that he loved her deeply made her feel a whole lot better—
what else mattered? 'I'm not sure what you're saying—
what you're asking,' she had to confess.

'I'm saying, my darling,' Joel began, with that serious,
not to say stern look still about him, 'that I don't want a
home-life where the minute I come into a room you go out
from it. I'm saying that I don't want a home-life where you
go and visit your grandfather at the weekend and leave me
wanting you back here so badly that I have to come after
you.'

'Oh, Joel!' she cried. 'Was that how it was?'

'I couldn't believe that in so short a time the apartment
felt alien without you in it,' he answered. 'I'm saying that,
without being aware of why, I had never felt happier than
when you finally agreed to marry me, and that I know now
the reason for that has nothing whatsoever to do with the
chairmanship. I'm almost certain that I've secured the position, but it's insignificant without you. And, while I know
that you have a true and ingrained aversion to anything
resembling a permanent marriage, I'm saying, my true love,
that I just cannot endure living through the next twenty-
three months expecting at the end of that time to receive
some notification telling me that you have instigated divorce proceedings.'

'Joel!' She cried his name in surprise—only he misread her surprise and took it for alarm.

'I know we agreed only two years—I know it, I know it,' he said hurriedly. 'But I love you so desperately I just cannot bear the thought of having to part from you. I can't promise you a life without upsets, but I promise here and now that never will I allow anything to harm you or put our marriage in jeopardy.' He looked deeply into her serious large green eyes. 'I love you, Chesnie Cosgrove Davenport. With all of my heart I love you. Would you,' he began, 'do me the honour of being my wife—permanently?'

'Oh, Joel,' she cried tremulously—she loved him, he loved her; what else mattered? 'I'd like nothing better,' she whispered huskily.

'You will? You'll stay married to me?' he insisted.

'Willingly,' she answered, and as a look of supreme joy at once came over his expression Joel hauled her close up against him.

'Oh, my dear, darling,' he breathed. 'Thank you,' he added on a heartfelt sound, and kissed her.

Do you like stories that get *up close* and *personal*?
Do you long to be loved *truly, madly, deeply...*?

If you're looking for emotionally intense, tantalizingly
tender love stories, stop searching and start reading

Harlequin Romance®

You'll find authors who'll leave you breathless, including:

Liz Fielding
Winner of the 2001 RITA Award for
Best Traditional Romance
(The Best Man and the Bridesmaid)

Day Leclaire
USA Today bestselling author

Leigh Michaels
Bestselling author with 30 million
copies of her books sold worldwide

Renee Roszel
USA Today bestselling author

Margaret Way
Australian star with 80 novels to her credit

Sophie Weston
A fresh British voice and a hot talent!

Don't miss their latest novels, coming soon!

HARLEQUIN®
Makes any time special®

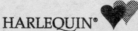
HINTMAG

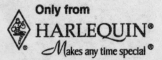